Sit down,
something I'
MOYA

'It's a pity Mum's going to kill me when she finds out – but I just know Morris is right for her.'

Mum's been on her own for far too long, so Hatty decides to find her a new man. And when she reads his ad in the personal column, it stands out like a flower in a garden of weeds. So what if her mother isn't interested right now? She will be, sooner or later.

Straightaway Hatty writes to Morris, pretending to be her mother, and soon letters are flying between them. But then comes the terrible moment of truth . . .

A wickedly funny, nail-biting story of madcap misadventure.

Sit down, Mum, there's something I've got to tell you

MOYA SIMONS

Puffin Books

Puffin Books
Penguin Books Australia Ltd
487 Maroondah Highway, PO Box 257
Ringwood, Victoria 3134, Australia
Penguin Books Ltd
Harmondsworth, Middlesex, England
Viking Penguin, A Division of Penguin Books USA Inc.
375 Hudson Street, New York, New York 10014, USA
Penguin Books Canada Limited
10 Alcorn Avenue, Toronto, Ontario, Canada M4V 3B2
Penguin Books (N.Z.) Ltd
182–190 Wairau Road, Auckland 10, New Zealand

First published by Penguin Books Australia, 1995

3 5 7 9 10 8 6 4 2

Typeset in 11/14 pt Bookman by Midland Typesetters
Made and printed in Australia by Australian Print Group

National Library of Australia
Cataloguing-in-Publication data:

Simons, Moya, 1942-   .
Sit down, Mum, there's something I've got to tell you.

ISBN 0 14 037552 X.
I. Title.

A823.3

For the other Morris

Chapter One

Saturday morning. School holidays. Mum is sitting at the breakfast table in her spotted PJS. I am sitting opposite her watching a beetle scurry towards the sugar bowl. Life is full of uncertainty. Do I kill it – thereby wiping out generation after generation of future beetles? I mean, who knows? One might be a special beetle destined to lead insects out of the dark age into the brave new world of tomorrow.

While I think about this Mum suddenly says, 'Sometimes I get lonely.'

I stop squinting at the beetle and look at my mum. She is staring at the opposite wall on which there is nothing but a picture of Aunt Harriet after whom I was named. Mum has a faraway look on her face.

'But I'm here,' I protest. 'Hey, me, remember?'

I smile charmingly at my mum. She glances briefly at me and sighs. I thought I was irresistible. What is she on about?

'You know, Hatty,' she says and her fingers play with her cereal spoon. 'I sometimes miss, well, having a man around. Since your father, um, left . . .'

Mum's eyes gaze past me, past Aunt Harriet's framed frown to the lounge room. I know. I don't have to turn around. I've seen that look before.

'It's that rotten urn on the mantelpiece,' I say. 'I mean, it's not as though Dad *died*. He just um, re-married. Why did you have to plonk earth in the urn from our old garden. It only makes you miserable.'

'Your father . . .' Mum says.

'Dad and you split up,' I reply. 'He's got on with his life. Don't you reckon it's time you got on with yours? I mean, there he is re-married and living in New Zealand and here you are with an urn full of earth on the mantelpiece. It's been five years you know. And look at me? I'm not whingeing and maladjusted even though I don't get to see him much. Honestly . . .'

I look back at the table. The beetle has disappeared. He's probably inside the sugar bowl gorging himself. If I swallow him when I put sugar in my tea will I die a horrible death? Death by beetlemitosis? Sounds good, huh?

'You're right, Hatty,' Mum says. She sniffs at nothing in particular. 'That's just what I've

2

been thinking about lately. It's been years and years and I should get on with my life. I'm not bad looking, am I? I'm not that old. Maybe I could still meet someone.'

I look at Mum in her PJS. There's cream on her face, her nose is red and her brown curly hair looks like millions of little wriggly worms out for a picnic.

'You look great,' I say.

After breakfast I stand in front of the large framed photograph of my Great Aunt Harriet. There she is with a sour expression on her face, arms folded, wearing her nurse's uniform.

'Now, she was some woman,' Mum says to me between sips of tea. 'Really feisty. And a truly wonderful nurse. It was a pity the way things ended for her . . . ' Mum's voice trails off.

My Great Aunt Harriet. My late grand-mother's older sister. Why couldn't she have had a name like Samantha or Deborah or anything but Harriet? It's not fair that I ended up with an off name like Hatty.

Aunt Harriet frowns at me from behind the glass in the frame. According to family rumour, without her Hitler's armies would have taken over Australia. Actually, though, Aunt Harriet didn't see any real *action*. I mean, she wasn't lying in a trench reloading a gun.

Nor was she flying a one-engine plane over Germany or plotting to kill rotten Hitler. She landed in Europe just after the war ended and worked for the Red Cross in hospitals. She must have seen some horrible things.

The real tragedy of Aunt Harriet is the way she died. You would have thought she'd have come back to Australia, her face creased with emotional suffering after all she'd seen. The Prime Minister would have given her a medal. There would have been a big parade through George Street with people throwing streamers and cheering.

It didn't happen that way. One night after a post-war party where everyone got tipsy, she stepped in front of a moving tank.

Poor, flattened Aunty Harriet.

We clean up the breakfast mess. Mum goes to have a shower and I grab the phone.

And dial Suzy's number.

She answers. I am grateful because her mum is always carrying on that I phone too often.

'It's me,' I say. 'What are we doing today?'

'Nothing,' Suzy groans. 'My family are going to the Blue Mountains for the day. I *tried* to tell my mum and dad that hey, I'm fourteen, I don't want to go on family outings. Dad gave me one of his long looks. Anyway, I've got to go, or I'll be given the silent treatment.'

So that's my Saturday. Fouled up by Suzy's parents' need for family togetherness.

What a rotten start to the summer holidays. It's early January and weeks of sunshine are stretched in front of me. Mum's just beginning her annual break from work. The two of us will have to take up knitting if I don't think of something soon.

When I get off the phone I dump myself onto the sofa, which is freckled by morning light. I punch a few cushions into shape, curl myself up and grab our morning paper which Mum has just collected from outside the front door. I flick through all the depressing news. I am so bored that I end up reading the ads.

It must be fate that I find myself studying the personal column. Amazing! The page is filled with ads from people looking for partners. Does Mum know about this?

'Hey, Mum,' I call out. 'Have you thought about putting an ad for a guy in the personal column in the newspaper? I bet you'd get heaps of guys wanting to meet you.'

Mum pokes her head around the corner of the door. 'I'd never, never put an ad in the paper.'

'Okay, just asking.'

I study the ads.

> 'TALL GOOD-LOOKING MAN WITH BIG MUSCLES
> WANTS TO MEET PETITE BLONDE AGED UP TO
> 40 YEARS FOR FUN TIMES.'

What does he mean by 'fun times'? Hey, I've got to protect my mum. I read further. Some ads are really off. Some are pathetic.

> 'ACTIVE 75 YEAR OLD HARD OF HEARING MALE
> WANTS TO MEET ATTRACTIVE, SLIM, SEXY,
> WELL-SPOKEN, INTELLIGENT, FINANCIALLY
> INDEPENDENT WOMAN AGED UP TO 35 YEARS.
> VIEW MARRIAGE.'

Is he kidding?

Then I find an ad that's different. In a garden of weeds it blooms as the only flower.

> 'I AM A LONELY MAN AGED 43. I WOULD
> VERY MUCH LIKE TO CORRESPOND WITH A
> WOMAN AGED UP TO ABOUT 45. I AM 180 CM
> TALL OF MEDIUM BUILD WITH LIGHT BROWN
> HAIR AND BLUE EYES. I LIKE CLASSICAL
> MUSIC AND READING CONTEMPORARY
> AUSTRALIAN LITERATURE. I ENJOY WRITING
> POETRY AS A HOBBY. IS THERE A LADY
> OUT THERE WHO'D LIKE TO WRITE TO ME?
> MY AIM IS TO CORRESPOND, EXCHANGE
> PHOTOGRAPHS AND, WHO KNOWS, MAYBE
> SOME DAY WE CAN MEET. PLEASE WRITE TO

This is exciting stuff! He sounds a bit shy but then so's Mum. He likes to write poetry. Okay.

Mum may not write poetry but I've seen her read it. He likes to read. Okay. Mum's not heavily into contemporary Australian literature. But she's thumbed through some thick books, and she's actually been to see *The Merchant of Venice* because she wanted to. I know that sounds a bit sick, but there you are.

He wants to write first, because obviously he doesn't like to rush things. Terrific! Mum's taken five years to decide it's time to get going. He sounds just her type.

'Mum,' I yell. 'I've found a guy for you. He sounds really cool. And there's no pressure at all. You don't even have to meet him. He just wants someone to write to. Come and have a read.'

Mum comes into the lounge room. The cream's off her face. She's looking not too bad for an almost forty-year-old mum. Mum could lose a bit of weight, but then so could I. Her skin's smooth. Her hair? Well, she should straighten it. I keep telling her, but she won't listen.

'Hatty, there is no way, no way I am going to reply to an advertisement in the personal column of the newspaper.' I try to butt in but Mum waves her hand at me. 'Now I appreciate your concern, but I can manage my own life, thank you very much. I've got my friends and my job.' Mum stops to think. 'I may join a club. You know, one of those clubs for single parents.'

I scowl. 'That's plain stupid and risky. You never know who you'll meet there. You're my mum. I've got to look out for you. Won't you read this ad? This guy sounds refined and kind of nice. He's heavily into literature and very shy.'

'And I suppose that's why he put an ad in the newspaper,' clucks Mum. 'I don't want to talk about this any more. Anyway, I'm going up the road to do some shopping. Want to come?'

'Not unless I have to.'

Mum mutters something about just buying a bit of this and that. Reassured that I won't have to take a guilt trip about her arms dropping off from carrying too much, I wave her goodbye.

Now, the guy who's written this ad really sounds like he has something going for him. If I was twenty years older I'd think about him for myself. He deserves a reply. I mean – what harm can it do if I answer on behalf of my mother? I can list all her good points.

I can send that photograph of us both standing outside the Opera House. I look great and Mum looks reasonably attractive and definitely intelligent. And I can use Suzy's address for the time being for him to write back.

There's no doubt about it. I am a real comfort to my mum.

I take out a pen and paper.

Dear Morris,

I saw your advertisement this morning in the newspaper and felt compelled to reply.

My name is Margaret and I am thirty-nine years old, but people tell me I look younger. I am divorced with a kind and intelligent daughter called Harriet (Hatty for short).

We live in Bondi in a small house and I work in an importing office doing secretarial work. However, in my spare time, I like to write poetry, and I just love to read.

I enjoy Shakespeare and Jackie Collins so you can see that my interests in literature are quite varied. I also like to visit the Art Gallery and the Opera House and I quite like ballet music.

I am sending you a photograph of me outside the Opera House. I hope you like it. I am better looking than the photograph. The cute-looking person beside me is my daughter, Hatty.

Well, this is all for now. I hope you will reply to this.

Yours sincerely, (no cross this out)

Yours, (no, yuk, he might get the wrong idea)

Warm regards, (yes, that's it!)

Margaret (Duncan)

I read and re-read my letter. Short and sweet but a masterpiece. A true, fair dinkum masterpiece.

I quickly write Suzy's address at the top of the letter and put it into an envelope.

Later, when Mum has returned and is talking to her best friend, Rosie, on the phone, I nick out.

I buy a stamp at the post office and send the letter on its way.

Honestly, I make the world a better place.

Chapter Two

On Sunday I head over to Suzy's house. Past the corner shop, turn right at the traffic lights. Second house along Bottlebrush Parade.

Suzy's arguing with her brother on the front lawn.

'No, you little nerd. I won't take you to the pictures. I wouldn't be caught dead with you.'

Suzy's brother, William, or Weasel as we call him, is stamping on Suzy's feet. Suzy is screaming and threatening his life.

Weasel is grinning. He's seven. Some of his teeth fell out naturally. Others got knocked out when he fell off his skateboard. When he laughs the inside of his mouth looks like the Jenolan Caves. Right now, he's laughing.

'You've *got* to take me to the pictures, or you can't go to the party Saturday. That's what Mum said. Ha, ha.'

Then he sees me. 'G'day, Fatty Hatty.'

'How's things, Weasel?'

'I hear Mum calling you,' says Suzy and Weasel gives me a toothless smile and runs inside.

'I'd like to mutilate him,' says Suzy.

We sit on her brick fence with the sun shining on us. The sky is clear. Tufts of cloud wander across it like happy marshmallows, which makes me think of food. Unfortunately, I am always hungry.

'How were the Blue Mountains?'

'You know – blue.'

'And those cute peaks – what are they called? – The Three Fingers?'

'The Three Sisters, you dope. Weasel got so excited he nearly fell over the fence at the lookout. Imagine, it would have been renamed The Three Sisters plus the One Brother.'

We swing our legs. Suzy has slim legs. They're brown. She's got long straight fair hair and no zits.

Now me. I've got filled out pale legs (okay – they're slightly plump), brown hair and a zit that keeps coming back on the top of my forehead. Fortunately it's only little. I occasionally talk to it and tell it not to bring any of its brothers or sisters to live on my forehead or I'll do something drastic (like get it transplanted to an armpit where the view and scent is definitely not interesting).

'Giles Conrad invited me to his birthday

party next Saturday,' says Suzy. 'He said you can come too if you like.'

Giles Conrad. Number one guy. King of the cool cats. Tall, dark-haired, great body. And about to turn sixteen. The guy's amazing. Going into year ten. A year ahead of Suzy and me. And he wants *us* to come to his party.

'Wow! I guess my mum will say it's okay.'

'His parents are staying home just to check that we kids don't vandalise the place,' says Suzy. 'My dad said he'll give us a lift. I've begged him to park a street away. It's going to look pathetic if he drops us at the door. He said he'll pick us up at eleven o'clock. Maybe we can wait outside so no-one sees him.'

My heart thumps like a drum. I hope Suzy can't hear it. She may be my best friend, but I just don't know how to tell her I have this thing for Giles. Anyway, he asked *her* to the party. I'm just an afterthought. Unless, maybe, just maybe he was too shy to ask me personally. This thought makes me smile.

Shy people! The salt of the earth. Like, what's-his-name, Morris. My mother's intended, except she doesn't know it yet.

'You may get a letter in the post addressed to my mum,' I tell Suzy.

Suzy squints at me. 'How come your mum wants to use our address?'

I tell Suzy about my clever plan to get my

mum back into action. Suzy smiles.

'Your mum would flip if she knew what you were doing. Still, I guess writing letters is pretty safe. I reckon you can tell a lot by what people say in letters. What do I tell my parents if something comes for your mum?'

'Um, just tell them that our letterbox has been wrecked or something like that. They don't see her often, so they won't check it out, and anyway, once I'm sure this Morris character is on the level I'm going to come clean.'

'Want a jelly baby?' Suzy fishes in her pocket and pulls out a paper bag. 'Have a good look,' she says. 'I bought them at a new shop down at the mall. They're boy and girl jelly babies.'

I look closely at the assortment of tiny multi-coloured jelly babies my best friend has put into the palm of my hand. I look really closely. She's right.

'How wonderfully obscene,' I say, swallowing a handful.

When I get home Mum's sitting in the lounge room by the phone yacking to Rosie. She's fidgeting around on the chair, like she can't find a comfortable position.

'All right. I'll do it. I know. You don't have to keep carrying on. I'll go. It's time I got my act together.'

When she gets off the phone I notice that her

cheeks are pink and her eyes are gleaming.

'I'm going to a singles' party,' she tells me. 'Next Saturday night. With Rosie. She's been at me for years to go out.'

Mum looks at the urn. I look at the urn. It stares back at us from its spot on the mantelpiece. It's a bleak dull oval-shaped copper container with a presence of total misery about it.

'Want to throw out the earth?' I ask.

'Um, not quite yet, Hatty. And don't ask me why. Not all questions have an answer. I'll know when it's right to get rid of the earth.'

Mum's eyes lose that gleam, and she stares at some vacant spot on the wall.

I march into the kitchen. Aunt Harriet glares down at me from her perch on the wall.

'Well,' I say to her. 'Just because you thought you had to bury yourself in nursing after your broken engagement, let me tell you there are others who think differently. Mum and me for instance. Do you know that we are both going to parties on the same night? Do you hear that, Aunt Harriet?'

Aunt Harriet's frown deepens. Hey – but it does! I could swear it.

'What's that you're saying dear?' Mum calls out. 'You're not talking to that photograph of your dead aunt again, are you?'

'If you can hang on to an urn full of earth,

15

then I can talk to Aunt Harriet. Anyway, as I was telling Aunt Harriet, I'm going to a party next Saturday night. Giles from school is going to be sixteen. His parents will be home so don't worry about me going wild, and Suzy's dad is giving me a lift both ways.'

Mum comes into the kitchen. She asks me three million questions about Giles and the party. She offers three million pieces of advice. I try to look interested. Then she gives me a hug.

'It sounds like it will be a very nice party, dear,' she says and her face goes soppy and melancholy. 'How the years fly. Now, we're like two women each about to conquer the world.'

'Heck, Mum, it's just Giles' birthday party,' I say, feeling embarrassed. 'Anyway, you'd better watch out. You know what happens at singles' parties. You've got to be really careful. It's not that I don't like your pal, Rosie, but let's face it. She's been around. You're still kind of naive. You don't know the scene. Lots of things have happened since Dad and you were together. AIDS for instance.'

Mum turns bright red.

'Thank you very much, Hatty, but I can look after myself. Anyway, I'm talking about going to a party, not having um, having um, a um, relationship.' My mother tosses her head to one side, sticks her nose in the air and walks out the room. 'I'm going to read a book.'

I want to tell her that, hey, Morris is the one. He's shy and also heavily into books. He won't rush you. He doesn't even want to meet you for ages. But if I tell her what I've done, there is a good chance I'll be grounded until I'm too old to appreciate parties.

So I return to the kitchen.

'Aunt Harriet, what was your life like, huh? You must have really loved that fiancé of yours to have turned your back on men. Not that you weren't a terrific nurse. But you could have had a boyfriend and been a nurse. Did that ever occur to you?'

Mum calls out from the depths of the house. 'Hatty, stop talking to that photograph.'

I stare at Aunt Hatty. Her face is square-shaped and stubborn. Her chin juts out defiantly. She looks like a cranky nun.

'People shouldn't bury themselves away,' I tell her. 'Mum shouldn't keep an urn filled with garden soil on our mantelpiece to remind her of happier times. She's got to get on with life. I *know* you were a great nurse. But I think you were running away.'

Is it my imagination or do the corners of Aunt Harriet's lips suddenly sag? If I didn't know better I'd say she looked like she was going to cry.

What was in the jelly babies Suzy gave me?

Chapter Three

Lazy days pass by. I write a letter to my dad in New Zealand. Suzy and I go down to Bondi Beach. The sun is sitting in the bright sky like a newly fried egg. The beach is packed and brightly coloured beach umbrellas dot the sand like confetti. Small kids stand around trying to eat ice-cream before it melts on them. We hang around the water's edge flaunting our voluptuous bodies. No-one seems to notice.

Unfortunately, the good weather doesn't last and by Thursday it's raining. Mum is in bed with a cold. Her face looks like a plate of runny jelly. Her eyes are like two sad little raisins.

'Go to the thops, therth a good girl, and bring me back thum athprin.' Mum's voice comes to me through a thick fog of nasal yuk.

So I go to the shops minus my raincoat and umbrella, because, 1. I look gross in them, and 2. it's a challenge to see how little rain will soak me before I reach cover.

I come home with asprin and eucalyptus

drops to soothe my mum's throat. I also come home soaking wet having proven that if rain pours down at five million drops a second and I run at a metre a second, it is a scientific certainty I shall arrive home half drowned.

I dry myself off and change before going in to see mum. She is lying on the bed in a miserable heap and her eyelids are like two swollen peaches.

'Have you brought me a glath of water with the athprin?'

I give my sick mum a glass of cool water and two asprin and three eucalyptus drops. I give myself four. Then I leave her because she says she wants to die in peace.

Mooching around the house, I try to decide who to call on the phone when the doorbell rings. I peek through the spyhole because you never know, it could be Jack the Ripper or worse. Fortunately, it's just Aunty Sandra.

Aunty Sandra is Mum's younger sister. She looks like Mum but is thinner. She lives with Uncle Michael and my two noisy cousins a few suburbs away.

I open the door.

'I brought your mum some vegetable soup. It'll help her cold,' says Aunty Sandra, giving me a kiss. The soup is probably very nutritious, but personally I prefer eucalyptus drops.

'Your face is dripping,' she comments.

'Pneumonia,' I say with courage, while I wonder where the hair dryer is. I take the big container of soup to the kitchen. Mum is calling out, 'Ith that you, Thandra?'

'Oh, and your mum thinks you should stop talking to that photograph in the kitchen,' says Aunty Sandra before she disappears into the sick room.

'Yeh, yeh.' I plonk myself on the sofa in the lounge room and stare at the window. The curtains are pulled back to ease the last bit of light in, and there's not much of that. The sky outside is heavily grey, and looks like it is suffering from deep depression. Huge blobby tears streak the window. The old gum tree throws itself about having a tantrum in the wind. I hug a small green cushion and wonder if the sun will ever come out again.

The phone goes. It's Suzy.

'Guess what? There's a letter here addressed to your mum. Who do you think it's from, huh?'

'Wow,' I say. 'This Morris guy is really keen. I'm coming over.'

I scream out to Mum that I'm just dashing out for a second, and before she has a chance to reply I'm gone. I tear down the road in my shorts and t-shirt. Past the shops. Turn right then right again and I'm outside Suzy's house. I run up to the door and press the buzzer urgently.

Weasel opens the door. 'You look like you've drowned, Fatty Hatty.'

'Let me in. Hi, Mrs Jacobs.'

Suzy's mum stands in the hallway frowning at me. 'Don't you own a raincoat, Hatty?'

Parents! They are all the same. I bet Aunt Harriet didn't own a raincoat. I bet when she went round Europe fixing all those sick people all she had was a thermometer, asprin and some eucalyptus drops.

Suzy runs up to me and we go to her bedroom. It's small and cluttered with books and ornaments and dried flowers in vases and photographs and posters of cuties and jewellery in boxes and out, and clothing lying inside her open wardrobe on the floor and on the back of her door and on her bed. Her mum won't clear it up. Neither will Suzy. Sometimes there's a faint smell in her room – like something is decomposing somewhere, but I guess unless she clears up the mess we'll never know.

I wipe rain away from my face with the end of her pink quilt, or maybe her pink skirt, while she opens the drawer of her desk and takes out from a huge clutter of paper a soggy ink-streaked letter.

'Here,' she says.

She pushes clothing off her bean bags and we sink into them while I fumble with the envelope.

Several neatly folded pages slide out.

'Quick, read it,' says Suzy. 'Oh, and what's that?'

A photograph falls out from between the pages. We both grab it.

'Hey, Morris is mine,' I scream. I peer at the picture I'm holding. Suzy leans against my shoulder.

'He's kind of, kind of . . .'

Morris is no Tom Cruise, but as far as older men go, I guess he's all right. He's wearing jeans and a striped shirt and is kneeling beside some flowers, holding a spade. Morris has light brown hair and an ordinary face. His smile is warm and his eyes are blue and friendly looking. He looks like an above-average middle-aged guy.

'He's okay,' I say finally.

Suzy nods her head. 'I reckon he's about right for her. Let's read the letter.'

I spread out the pages. Morris's handwriting is small and neat. His letter is on lined paper, and his writing is very close together and has an orderly look about it. I start to read.

Dear Margaret,

I was delighted to receive your letter. I did

get others, but your letter and photograph struck a chord in my heart. I think you are a very attractive lady, and your daughter is lucky enough to look just like you.

I pause. 'I *don't* look like my mum, do I?' 'Who cares?' says Suzy. 'Read on.'

    I like to see a woman with meat on her bones. I was also happy to know there is someone out there who enjoys reading books and writing poetry too.

    I hope you like my photograph. I am currently working as a gardener on a large farm in the country. My special hobby is the cultivation of new types of roses. Do you like gardening, Margaret?

    I am a serious-minded person. I enjoy home comforts and meaningful family life. I love classical music. I have just finished listening to *Swan Lake* on the radio. How special it is that you also love ballet music.

    I am hopeful that we can get together in the future and share our hobbies. We seem to have so much in common.

    Meantime, here is a piece of poetry I have written. Maybe you can send one back to me and we can exchange ideas.

If we could meet some time
beside some lovely place,
If I could get to know you
and see your pretty face,
We just might stand a chance, Marg,
we just might find we had
a special kind of friendship,
Now would that be so bad?

I await your reply.

   With best wishes and high hopes for our
future,

Morris

Suzy has buried her face in her hands. She
is making awful spluttering noises.

'Hey,' I say, 'it may not be Henry Lawson, but
the guy's got class.'

'That's the worst poem I've ever heard,' says
Suzy.

Mrs Jacobs comes into the room. I quickly
put the letter to one side.

'Want to stay for lunch?' she asks me.

'No thanks. I'd better get home.'

'I'll lend you an umbrella if I can safely find
my way out of here,' says Mrs Jacobs glaring
at Suzy. She backs carefully out of the room.

'No way,' I mutter, tucking the letter inside
my pocket after she's gone. 'I'm off. I've got to

get home and write something hot to Morris to keep the flame alive.'

'Your mum would just freak out if she knew what you were up to,' Suzy says, smiling wickedly.

'I have her interests at heart.'

'Don't worry about an umbrella, Mrs J,' I call out and before she has a chance to reply I have taken off.

I'm running down the road at super speed. I'm dashing small waterfalls falling off trees. I'm skidding along the pathway. Down this road, up that one, why does my stomach bounce . . . I'm home!

I open the front door quietly and slip inside. I can hear my mother's voice.

'I jutht hope I'm better by Thaturday. The day Rothie takes me to my firtht thingleth party.'

'You'll be fine,' Aunty Sandra says encouragingly.

'I'm back,' I shout out, and then I'm sorry I even said I was going anywhere, because the two of them carry on about how I run around never saying where I'm going and so on.

In my bedroom I dry off. Suzy and I may be physical opposites but when it comes to managing our bedrooms we are true soul mates. My room is a tapestry of confusion. There are books on top of books underneath underwear above skirts. There are hangers lying on pencils behind empty cans of lemonade and chocolate wrappers . . .

However, there is one place I keep clear. My dressing table. Even a slob has standards. Here I keep those precious bottles of perfume guaranteed to stun on impact, lipstick (hand-me-downs from Mum), important magazines about how to become and stay forever beautiful, zit cream, hair mousse and a trillion necessities like beads and bracelets and save the whale badges.

In my top dressing table drawer, in neat stacks, are letters from ex and current penfriends from remote parts of the world and cuttings from magazines considered essential for existence. Like how to lengthen your eyelashes by adding parsley to your diet and things like that. I also have some old floral notepaper given by someone sometime as a gift. Finally I can put it to good use. I take out a sheet of paper and dab perfume all over it. Good. It smells like a bunch of gardenias.

My pen is poised . . .

Dear Morris,

I received your letter and I'm writing back straightaway. How kind of you to notice how attractive my daughter and I are.

Your photograph inspired me to write the following poem.

I stop writing and bite the end of my pen. Inspiration, where are you?

I put the pen down and run into the kitchen. There are still all those breakfast dishes to wash up. Oh well. I take some ice-cream from the freezer, put it in a bowl and add some chocolate sauce, sit down, push a few smelly dishes to one side and happily gorge myself.

Our kitchen is cosy. There are Mum's little friendly magnets all over the fridge with reminders to do this and that. There are the buttercup-coloured curtains either side of the window and happy pot plants lined up in a row on the window ledge.

It's a friendly place. Well, almost. As I am lifting my spoon, Aunt Harriet frowns down at me.

'Well, what are you looking at?' I ask her. 'I'm a growing girl. I *need* energy. I've got to write a poem. A soppy poem for Morris.'

Aunt Harriet's frown deepens.

'So, you don't approve, huh? You reckon I should stay out of Mum's life? Well, I reckon if someone would have been around to give you some advice you wouldn't have buried yourself in nursing. You can't throw your life away on one failed romance, Aunt Harriet.

Mum's never really got over Dad. And the singles' party she's going to isn't the answer. Everyone *knows* what goes on there. I'm just doing my duty. I've got to watch out for her.'

'Hatty?' Aunty Sandra comes into the kitchen. Her curly hair is just like Mum's but wrigglier. 'Stop talking to that stupid photograph.'

I don't answer. She wouldn't understand. I don't even understand.

'And you've got a white moustache. Don't you think you eat too much?'

'*Hurumph*,' I answer, my mouth full.

Later, when Aunty Sandra has gone back to sit with my mother and I have my physical and mental energy restored by the ice-cream, I go back to my bedroom.

I fiddle with my pen for a while, wondering things like who made the very first pen and who wrote the very first poem. Finally, I write this for Morris.

> *I think you could be*
> *the man for me.*
> *But it's hard to say*
> *when you're far away.*
> *If we could meet*
> *it'd be a real treat.*
> *When I get over the flu*
> *we'll see what we can do.*

There! It's not too much of a come on. And I know, I just know this Morris character has *true soul*. I'm quite sure that when he finally suggests a meeting my mum will be overcome with joy and she'll appreciate the effort I've gone to.

I write a few other bits and pieces to Morris. Then I sign myself,

Your dear friend,

Margaret

I'll post the letter later. Now, I have to think of other things. Like – what am I going to wear Saturday night?

Life is so hectic.

Chapter Four

By Saturday morning Mum's nose is dry and so is the weather. The sky is blue with a dab of clouds. I've ironed my jeans and washed my hair, which is (when I hold my head high) past my shoulders. It is so clean it squeaks its appreciation. Mum shows me the dress she wants to wear for her debut into the 'real world'.

'What do you think, Hatty?'

The dress is a blinding shade of red. My mum will resemble a traffic light. The guys will need sunglasses to look at her. The dress is also daggy because Mum hasn't been anywhere in years. It's too short, there are too many buttons and the belt is all wrong. But I can't tell her that. It's too late for anything but . . .

'You'll knock 'em dead.'

'Hmm . . .' says Mum and she raises her skinny winged eyebrows at me. 'I just want to look okay. I'm not actually looking for a boyfriend, Hatty.'

'Hah!' I comment. You don't have to worry about a thing, I think to myself. Good old poetic Morris is coming your way. I sidle off to my bedroom.

I try on my jeans. I don't look too bad. It's true they're a bit tight, but if I hold my breath part of the time and don't overeat before tonight I should get away with it.

What was it that my friend Morris said? He likes a woman with 'meat on her bones'. The man has taste. I just hope Giles and the other boys at the party feel the same way. My hair is quite shiny. My eyes are a decent shade of hazel. My cheeks are rather full, but that doesn't matter. It gives me a healthy look, and no-one can ever suggest that I am anorexic. Okay. I might not be Elle MacPherson, but I reckon I'm at least average.

In a while I wander down to the shops to get Giles' birthday gift. I buy him a silver pen in a velvet case and a funny card. On the front of the card is a huge bear waving a sign: 'Whatever you do, don't open this card if you'd like $10,000.' Inside it reads: 'Well, I *did* warn you.'

I would have liked to have bought him a card with a more personal message. One that said something like, 'to a cool cat from a hot friend', but I don't have the guts.

Time passes as slowly as a snail on crutches. I phone Suzy four times just to check in and try to be supportive to my mum who keeps running to the toilet because she says she's nervous.

'Did you hear that?' I say to Aunt Harriet on my way to the fridge. '*She's* nervous. I'm the one going to Giles Conrad's party.'

Aunt Harriet maintains a stony silence as she watches me, her starched hat firmly in place, her eyes steely.

When the sun finally calls it a day and the sky is deep purple, Mum and I go to our respective bedrooms to make ourselves beautiful. Later we collide in the bathroom. Mum is wearing her white bathrobe, and her face is shining with some gunk which she is using to soften her skin before she covers it with other gunk. All this is to make her beautiful.

I am almost ready. I just need half an hour or so in the bathroom to spray my hair and stare at myself because the light in the bathroom is rather soft and it somehow makes you look really cool even if you aren't. Mum needs time to study her reflection too, so we argue about who goes first and of course, she wins.

Meantime the house struggles to breathe as the potent smells of 'Midnight in Paris'

(Mum's) and 'Temptation' (mine) fog the air.

At seven o'clock the doorbell rings. Suzy has arrived. We stare at each other. She looks great in black jeans and a top.

'You look terrific,' I say.

'I look terrible,' she mutters. 'But in this bag I have lots of make-up. *They* wouldn't let me put it on. When Dad drops us off I'll fix my face up.'

I've only got on eyeshadow and pale pink lipstick. What a lucky break. We'll both look fantastic.

Mum comes to the door, dress rustling, high heels clicking.

'Mrs Duncan. You look, you look . . . ' Suzy gasps.

'Oh, thank you, Suzy,' Mum says. 'And you look very nice too.'

Mum wishes us both a good time. She tells me to be careful. I tell her to be careful. She sees us to the gate and waves hello to Suzy's dad who waves back. Suzy and I run out to where her dad waits in his car.

'Your mum looks like a traffic light,' says Suzy.

Poor Mum!

Suzy's dad looks at me, sniffs, says, 'That smell's enough to give me hay fever, Hatty,' and off we go. He makes small talk about:

1. I assume there's not going to be any grog.

2. Don't leave the party for any reason.

3. I'm coming at eleven o'clock sharp. Be ready.

4. Are you sure his parents are going to be home?

Suzy replies: 'No' – 'No' – 'Yeh' – 'Yeh' in that order. She nudges me in the back seat. 'He's driving me nuts.'

As we approach Giles' house she says, 'Dad, drop us just here. Don't pull up outside. It's just not done.'

'I don't care what's done,' says Suzy's dad. 'I want to check that his parents are staying home. Stop making those horrible noises. I'm checking and that's that.'

'Terrific,' groans Suzy.

So we park near the house and the three of us get out of the car. Giles' house is decked out like a Christmas tree. A row of coloured lights hang across the front porch. Kids are spilling out of the house into the garden which is large and from what I can see full of shrubs and garden beds. Through the open windows you can see kids dancing and it's all looking very good.

'This is so off. Everyone will see you, Dad. I can't believe this,' says Suzy. 'How can you do this to me?'

'Stop carrying on,' says her dad.

I just walk alongside them. I don't have a

resident dad, though he does write and I'll get to see him next school holidays. It would be nice if he lived in Sydney, but I don't know how Mum would cope now he's re-married. Sometimes I miss him a lot. Even though he'd probably carry on like Suzy's dad is carrying on right now.

We get to the front door, which is wide open. Lots of kids are hanging around in the hallway, and I can hear music and see kids in the front room throwing themselves around like twitching gorillas. Suzy's dad stands near the door while Suzy, who is embarrassed beyond words, goes to find Giles' parents. I study all the cuties.

'Hi, Hatty,' says one school creep.

I nod. I won't even answer. I'm saving all the words in my brain for Giles.

Giles' mother comes to the door with Suzy. She's tall and friendly looking. She spends a few minutes with Suzy's dad reassuring him that his beloved daughter is in safe hands. Suzy's dad asks a few more mortifying questions while Suzy shifts from one foot to another. Her dad then wishes us a good time. Suzy says, 'Yeh, yeh, yeh' and heaves a huge sigh of relief when he finally leaves.

'Honestly, we're fourteen. You'd think he'd trust me,' she says indignantly. 'Come on, let's go straight to the bathroom and we can pile on some make-up.'

We bump into Giles on the way. Suzy and I quickly wish him the best birthday and drop his presents into his arms, which are full with other gifts. Suzy holds one hand half across her face. She is obviously anxious that Giles does not see her naked face. Giles smiles and mutters something that sounds like thank you. Then he disappears with his loot.

We find the bathroom and Suzy takes out from a small bag an amazing assortment of make-up. Tubes of this, bottles of that, mascara, eyeliner, different shades of lipstick, blusher. Wow! We stand in front of a long, brightly lit mirror and large marble basin and get to work.

'My parents would freak out if they knew I had this stuff,' giggles Suzy.

Ten minutes later Elle herself would envy us. There is not a single feature on our faces which has not been made more beautiful by Suzy's make-up kit.

We saunter out of the bathroom looking fantastic. I lose Suzy because hey, we're here to look at the talent, not talk to each other. I dip a chip. I drink some green punch. I swivel my ample hips in time to the music. Where is Giles Conrad? A nerd from school comes over to me. Martin Lonnigan. He pushes his glasses up and down his nose nervously.

'Music's good, huh?'

'Yeh,' I say.

'What happened to your face?'

'Huh?'

'It's an awful colour.'

'Oh yeh?'

'Oh yeh!'

Suddenly I spy Giles. He's talking to Suzy and he has an arm on her shoulder. She's smiling and he's looking right into her eyes. I feel queasy inside.

There's no point kidding myself. He *likes* Suzy, my best friend, my soul mate, the one who runs to the letterbox to collect Morris's letters. What's worse is that she likes him. Look, she's fluttering her black lashes and flicking her hair back. I feel jealous, but it's not going to help, is it.

I've got to be brave. Who else is around? A skinny, dark-haired boy comes over to me.

'Want to dance?'

I don't know him. He's not cute but he's not awful. He's wearing jeans like almost everyone else, is tall and has a bony face. I notice one small zit just above his thick left eyebrow and wonder if my own is visible. Oh well.

We dance to the sounds of heavy rock and he starts to talk to me.

'I've just moved around here.' He swivels around me. The guy can actually dance. 'I live

37

next door. I'll be coming to your school next term.'

'Oh yeh,' I say. Giles Conrad has just whispered something to Suzy, my best friend, my soul mate. Now she's smiling. She's showing him two lines of toothpaste-white teeth.

'My name's Raymond.'

'I'm um . . . ' I hesitate. I must be in a bad way, because I can't at that moment remember my name. 'I'm Hatty,' I finally say.

'Do you know everyone here?' asks Raymond.

'Huh?' I ask. Out of the corner of my eye I have just seen Giles Conrad touch Suzy's cheek. On the other hand she could have some food there that he's kindly removing.

My feet jiggle around automatically. Raymond has given up on conversation and just continues to dance.

'Want some punch?' he says eventually.

I nod. Life is rapidly becoming miserable and perhaps a glass of punch would do me good. Raymond scoops punch from a huge bowl of green liquid in which slivers of oranges and cherries swim. We go out onto Giles' balcony, which has a view overlooking the city lights.

'Thanks.' I take a look at this guy, Raymond. The light's not good on the balcony but it's good enough to see that Raymond, though not exactly cute, definitely has a sensitive face. And that lonely zit. Just like mine. I feel a sense of bonding. I think of the photograph of Morris. *He* wasn't super cute, but he had a sensitive face.

'Do you ever write poetry?' I ask. Then I feel embarrassed because it's such a dumb question.

'Huh?' says Raymond. 'Sometimes. If I feel down, I might.'

Who needs Giles Conrad? I give Raymond my most appealing smile. I stare intently into his eyes.

'Do you write poetry?' he asks me.

'I wrote a poem just the other day,' I say. 'Do you like classical music – like, say um, *Swan Lake*?'

'No, I like jazz and blues. My dad plays the clarinet. He plays stuff from the thirties and forties. It's great.'

I suddenly get a picture of Aunt Harriet in my mind. She's dancing with her fiancé. Clinging to him while plaintive strains of old melodies trumpet through a crowded old-time dance hall. Her dress is made of satin and her fiancé has his hair parted through the middle and slicked down on both sides. His moustache curls slightly at the corners. They twirl past other couples. They hold each other tightly. They whirl past potted palms. They . . .

'I'd like to hear your dad play sometime,' I say.

'Um, maybe if you mean it, you can come over and watch when he rehearses with his band.'

I nod. This guy is cool. This could be the start of a new and wonderful friendship. I'll get over Giles Conrad in time.

The night moves quickly on. Savouries and drink are followed by the big birthday cake, the big birthday song and more food. Giles stands there and says it's the best birthday party he's had. Then he looks right at Suzy. I feel mildly depressed so I stuff myself. Raymond follows me around. He stuffs himself. He is skinny so it's okay. I am not skinny. I have meat on my bones. Lots of it.

Suddenly, while I am standing eating another helping of chocolate cake, I get this feeling of something being stretched to its limits. Then comes a tiny squeaky sound which only I can hear. It's coming from my jeans. They have split.

It is one of the wonders of life that at the same time my jeans split, the clock strikes eleven, and Suzy's dad appears asking for the return of his beloved daughter and her friend.

It is very difficult to walk backwards, but I do the best I can. I say see you soon to Raymond, having given him my phone number. I say goodbye to Giles and his parents, thanking them for the great time.

Suzy says goodbye to Giles and his parents, except that when she says goodbye to Giles her voice suddenly becomes husky and he gives her this special look and says, 'I'm glad you could come.' But he doesn't mean 'glad'. He means 'wildly excited', 'ecstatic', 'thrilled beyond description' and his eyes wander over Suzy like he has loose sockets.

Suzy's dad coughs then grabs Suzy and we leave.

'What a great party,' growls Suzy. 'Trust my dad to spoil things by coming so early. Hey, what's wrong with you? Why are you walking backwards?'

As I back out of the door, I point to the rear end of my jeans. Suzy can't stop laughing, though I don't think it's funny at all and what's more, my backside's getting cold.

Her dad drives me home. Another car pulls up just as I hop out. It's Mum. And she's looking like a happy traffic light. A man jumps out of the driver's seat and we all meet at the front gate.

'Joe, this is Hatty. Hatty, this is Joe,' says Mum, who is giggling like a kid.

I mumble something. Then this Joe creep disappears after telling Mum he'll be in touch.

Hey! What's going on here?

When Mum and I are inside the house I take a good look at her. She takes a good look at me.

'What's that appalling muck on your face, Hatty?'

'Who's that creep?'

'Where did you get that make-up from?'

'Are you going to go out with him?'

'You *know* how I feel about girls your age wearing so much make-up. You look awful.'

'You can't go out with the first guy that asks you.'

'Wash it all off and go straight to bed.'

'Mum, we've got to have a good talk in the morning. I want the lowdown on this Joe guy.'

'Did you hear what I said, Hatty?'

'Did you hear what I said, Mum?'

We carry on a bit more, give up, and then say good night.

Chapter Five

I n the morning the cat next door howls and wakes me up early. Apart from the cat howling, the birds, who are probably being chased by the howling cat, are chirping. The sun is out and I'm thirsty. I go into the kitchen and pour myself some juice.

'I had a great time last night, Aunt Harriet,' I tell her. 'Raymond has definite possibilities. Don't frown at me like that. I'm serious.'

Mum staggers into the room. She still has some of last night's mascara running down one cheek. Either that or Joe tried to knock her out. Her hair looks like, well, I'm just not going to say, and her dressing gown has been done up with all the wrong buttons.

'I'm aching all over, Hatty,' she tells me. 'I haven't danced that much since, since ...' She leaves the sentence unfinished and gets that far off look in her eyes which I can't stand.

'So, tell me about Joe,' I say. 'And don't leave

anything out. Then I'll tell you about Raymond.'

'Raymond, who's Raymond?'

'Tell me about Joe first.'

'I want to know about Raymond.' Mum's totally determined, so I have to tell her what I know. The way he likes jazz. The sensitive face. The fact that he can actually dance instead of just shuffling around.

'Da-dee-da-dum.' Mum sings some song I've never heard of and beats time with her fingers on the kitchen table. 'He sounds a nice boy.'

'And Joe?'

'He's a nice man.' Mum fills the kettle and continues to sing.

'Well?' I blurt out. 'Is that all you're going to tell me? That he's *nice*. Did he try to kiss you? Is he going to see you again?'

Mum giggles. 'Ha ha. No to the first question, yes to the second. Do you want tea or hot chocolate?'

I gasp. 'Mum, you *know* those singles' parties are just an excuse for men with one thing in mind to meet women. You're so naive.' I look at Aunt Harriet. 'You tell her how you've got to be careful. Tell her not to jump straight into another relationship.'

Aunt Harriet stares at us both with pursed lips.

'Stop that nonsense, Hatty,' says Mum. 'And

as for jumping into another relationship, it's been five years since your father went . . . '

'I know. So then, are you going to empty the earth in the urn? Has the time finally come?'

'Do you want vegemite on your toast?'

End of conversation.

The very next night, while Mum and I are watching an intense psychological thriller on TV, the phone rings. I grab it.

A male adult voice says, 'Is Margaret there?'

It's that Joe creep. I call Mum and she tries to look very casual when I say that it's a guy. She walks slowly over to the phone, picks it up, drops it, then retrieves it from the floor.

'What are you looking at?' she says to me. 'Go watch TV.'

Then she sits herself on the sofa and twirls the telephone cord around her fingers as she talks and giggles and giggles and talks. Not that I'm watching her closely. I mean, there's this guy on TV with a knife the size of a skateboard running around. Finally she puts the phone down.

'Do you reckon you'd be okay if I leave you for a while? Joe wants to take me out to the Leagues Club. We won't be gone long.'

'Of course I'll be okay. Kids of my age are already out baby-sitting,' I growl. This does not suit me at all. Gentle Morris with his

45

poetic soul could be very put out by this turn of events.

My mother springs into action. She runs out of the room like she's got a sudden attack of gastric. Soon I hear water being splashed around in the shower. A few minutes later, the smell of 'Midnight in Paris' fills the house and is enough to make my eyes water.

While the man with the huge knife on TV stalks his latest unsuspecting female victim, Joe, the new man in my mother's life, is probably stalking his. What if he's some kind of axe murderer? What if I never see my mum again? What if Aunt Harriet and I are destined to spend the rest of our lives together?

The doorbell rings. Mum shouts to me, 'Let Joe in. Offer him a cup of tea. I'll just be a sec.'

What rotten timing! Just when the psychopath is about to lunge forward and finally finish off his victim, Mum's date has arrived. I open the front door cautiously. Who is this guy? What's he up to? How can I be sure he's not just after my mother's body?

Joe stands there. He's holding a bunch of roses and looking nervous. He's wearing a suit, and a tie which has stripes running across it. He has quite a lot of lines on his face, bags under his eyes, and a small, worried smile.

'G'd evening, Hatty,' he says.

'Hi, um . . . come in,' I say.

Joe follows me down the hall and into the lounge room and I tell him to sit down and make himself at home. He sits on the edge of an armchair and his jaw begins to twitch. Of course that doesn't mean a thing. He could be anybody. Capable of anything . . .

'Won't be a moment, Joe,' my mum calls out.

'Want a cup of tea?' I ask him.

'No, thanks,' Joe says, nodding his head, which is curious and confusing. He looks around the room and eventually stares at the figures darting around the TV screen.

'Crikey,' he says, as the psychopath strikes again and again at a new victim. 'Should you be watching this stuff?'

I try to look profound as I reply. 'A recent study has shown that teenagers who watch horror movies are less likely to commit violent crime. Watching movies like this gives one a chance to act out inner conflict in a safe environment.'

Joe shifts around on his seat. The murderer on TV strikes again and again at the heart of his victim. Blood gushes everywhere. I eat popcorn.

'Phew,' says Joe. He takes out a neatly folded handkerchief and wipes his forehead. Mum appears. She doesn't look like a traffic light, thank goodness. More like a flouncing

47

daffodil. She's wearing her good yellow dress, and all this for, 'going to the Leagues Club with Joe'.

'You look great,' says Joe, and he fumbles with the flowers, then gives them to Mum.

'Oh, you shouldn't have bothered,' says Mum, while I wonder why adults are so hypocritical. 'You shouldn't have bothered' roughly translated means 'I love them. Buy me more, more, more'.

'You'll put these in a vase, won't you, Hatty?'

Even her Aussie accent suddenly has a refined edge to it. After five years of quiet suburban life with an urn on the mantelpiece, Aunt Harriet in the kitchen and a terrific daughter, my mum is coming unstuck over what's-his-name ... Joe.

Then Mum carries on dreadfully. She gives me the name of the Leagues Club they are going to, the phone number, and instructs me to page her if I so much as cough. She runs around checking if the windows are locked. Joe just stands there politely cracking his knuckles and smiling at me.

Finally she's satisfied. Mum gives me a hug and says goodbye. You'd think she was off on safari and not coming back for a few years.

I stick the flowers in a vase and go back to watching TV. Unfortunately, in the time it has taken for me to see Mum and Joe off, the cops have already closed in on the psychopath. He tries bravely to ward them off with his skateboard-sized knife, but unfortunately he is lost. A bullet to the chest and one to his head sends him into a frenzy of pain as he staggers, clutches himself and finally drops to the ground.

The phone rings. I lean over and pick it up.

'Hi, is Hatty home?'

I choke on popcorn. A male voice, strong and eager, is asking for *me*.

'Speaking,' I gasp.

'Um, this is Raymond. I was wondering if say, you'd like to come over to my place. My dad's group is going to rehearse. Ah, you said you'd be interested . . . '

'Sure,' I say. 'That'd be great. When?'

'How about Wednesday at six o'clock. Dad says he can run you home later. I can meet you at your place, if you like.'

We make arrangements. My heart thumps like a frenzied metronome.

Later, after watching the late news, I go to bed. Mum's not home. Shouldn't she be home? What do I do in these circumstances? Do I wait up for her? What are my responsibilities? Should I page her at the Leagues Club? This is a brand new situation.

Somehow, I fall asleep. I dream a muddled dream about Aunt Harriet. She's young and her hair is chestnut brown and falls in soft waves past her shoulders. Her eyes are bright and she's smiling at this guy and saying, 'Of course I'll marry you, Thomas. Of course.' He touches her shoulder. He kisses her cheek. He kisses her full on her large pink mouth. She looks so happy. Then another woman enters the dream. She's hard-looking with a skinny red mouth and a mole on her nose. I see Thomas looking at Aunt Harriet then at the woman with the mole on her nose. He can't make up his mind. Each woman grabs an arm and pulls. Thomas has to choose in a hurry. Unfortunately he likes women with moles on their noses. He says to Aunt Harriet, 'I'm sorry. If you even had a small wart, it would make all the difference, but as it is . . . it's no good, Harriet. I have to leave you.'

I wake up sweating and throw off my blankets. Where's Mum? I hear a car pull up outside, laughter, and Mum chiming, 'It was a lot of fun.'

What was a lot of fun? I curl up in bed. This is no good. I am fixing my mother up with her true soul mate, Morris. This is no good at all.

Chapter Six

The following few days see my mother changed from a wilting weed into a happy hydrangea. She's singing daggy songs around the house and cleaning as though she actually enjoys it. She changes the water in the vase containing Joe's flowers at least twice a day. She even cleans our light fittings, which means that a few spiders have been left totally homeless. Mum polishes the urn, occasionally opening it up, staring at the earth inside and saying 'Hmn'.

Meantime, Suzy phones me to say, 'Hey, what do you think of Giles Conrad? Is he right for me?'

I swallow a big lump which has risen like a camel's hump in my throat and say generously, 'He's nice. You two look great together.'

'He's asked me to go out ice-skating with him this week.'

So I tell her about Raymond and the jazz rehearsal. Suzy is very pleased. She sees our lives filled with double dates.

'He's Giles' next-door neighbour. It will almost be like we're going out with twins. This is great. By the way there's a letter here for your mum from what's-his-name.'

Morris the Mighty strikes again! I'm down but not out. I shall continue my efforts with Morris. I *know* the guy. This Joe creep, on the other hand, has shifty eyes, a twitching jaw and doesn't like my taste in TV programmes.

I leap into action, shout 'see you' to Mum and run all the way to Suzy's place. She's sitting waiting for me on her brick fence, chewing a blade of grass, the wind blowing her long hair. She takes the letter from out of her jeans pocket.

'Your letters must be doing things for Morris. He seems really keen.'

I smile at Morris's neat little handwriting on the slightly smudged envelope and tear it apart. I open the folded pages. Several tiny rose petals fall out. What a guy!

Suzy leans over my shoulder. I read:

Dear Margaret,

Your letter and your poem meant so much to me. If only my last wife had understood me the way you do. There seems to be a similarity in the way we think and feel that can only be called 'amazing'.

I have spent today cultivating my rose garden on the farm. Did you know that there is a rose named 'Margaret'? I grow this particular rose and now the name has taken on new meaning. I have also been tending a vegetable patch where I grow cabbages and carrots.

The farm, by the way, is fairly isolated, and surrounded by green rolling hills. In the morning the tops of these hills are covered in mist. Sometimes in winter we even get a slight sprinkle of snow. It is peaceful. I miss, however, the warmth of female companionship and it is my deepest hope that sometime we shall meet.

Tomorrow I shall be working on the repair of farm machinery. Life is very busy here, but I turn in early at night with you on my mind.

Write soon. Meanwhile, here is another poem. (Hope you like my efforts.)

Here in the country,
I spend many hours
tending the vegetables
and growing the flowers.

It gets lonely at times
then I think, Marg, of you
and that keeps me going,
Yes, Marg, it's true.

Suzy laughs. 'He's so corny. This guy is really stuck on you, sorry, your mum. You're getting in a bit deep, Hatty. What are you going to do if he suddenly comes to Sydney?'

'I'm going to tell Mum. I've just got to find the right time. Anyway, Morris won't just turn up. He'll let me know first, and then I can prepare Mum. He's right for her. You can tell by this poetry. It might sound soppy to you, but I think it shows true heart and commitment.'

'Well, if it ever does take off, I hope you like country life. Want to go down the beach later? We may have to take Weasel though.'

'Sure.'

I re-read Morris's letter on the way home and then tuck it safely in the bottom drawer of my desk. Mum pops in.

'I've only got a few more weeks off work,' she says. 'I feel like doing something different. How do you think I'd look with red hair?'

In my mind I see my mother with her new red hair wearing her red dress. She will look like a fire-engine.

54

'I don't think it's a good idea,' I say. 'Your brown hair is fine.'

'But I need a change, Hatty. It will give me a lift. Suddenly I feel young again.'

I sigh. Mum with red hair. I don't know. I wander into the kitchen. 'Hi, Aunt Harriet. How's things?'

Aunt Harriet winces at me. I think of my dream. I wonder about the man she loved. She must have loved him heaps to forget about all other men.

'Do you know anything about Aunt Harriet's fiancé, Mum?'

Mum squints up at Aunt Harriet. 'Only what I've told you before. Thomas was a dance instructor. They met when she went to learn ballroom dancing, in London in the late 1930s. Your aunt was just a beginner but he taught her to dance and she became so good they entered competitions together and won prizes. She was quite pretty really. I think Aunty Sandra may still have that old photograph belonging to your great-grandmother of the two of them. I'll ask her to bring it over. Anyway, as I've told you, he met this other woman.' Mum stops to think. 'It was after he'd become engaged to your great aunt. He realised it was a big mistake and tried to make up with Harriet, but she couldn't forgive him and decided to study nursing. She was wonderful. During the Blitz, when they dropped all those bombs on London, she worked round the clock in hospitals and then when peace was declared she went to Europe with the Red Cross. She nursed in makeshift hospitals there until that sad night when she got hit by that tank. Poor Aunt Harriet!'

'I'd love to see that photograph,' I say.

'I'll ask Aunty Sandra to have a look for it. Oh, and I'm going to the hairdresser later this morning. Don't look at me like that. My mind's made up.'

So later that morning Mum disappears from the house, and I fumble in my drawer for Morris's letter.

Dear Morris, I write.

A change is as good as a holiday, they say. So I've become a redhead. You do like redheads, don't you? My daughter, Hatty, tried to talk me out of it, but I did insist.

I was interested to hear about your life on the farm. It sounds so picturesque.

Here in Bondi summer life revolves around going to the beach and the movies, and odd visits to the Leagues

Club. The other night Hatty and I
watched this scary thriller on TV. You
should have seen the guy. He had a knife
that would have put 'Crocodile Dundee' to
shame. Do you like watching the
occasional horror movie? I know you have
a gentle nature, but I find that horror
films have a calming effect on me. I hope
you don't find this awful.

Now, my special poem for you.

I chew on my pen and study the sky outside
my window.

Today the sky is very blue
and the clouds are small and white.
The ocean's full of little waves
and my hair is very bright.

I'd like to walk on the beach with you
let our feet sink in the sand.
We could watch the tide come in
and you could hold my hand.

Write again to me soon.

Love,

Margaret

There, I've finally put the magic word 'love' in at the end. But I guess it's okay. It's not like this is a one-night stand. Morris and I have been writing to each other now for nearly two weeks.

I sprinkle the letter with perfume, stick it in a matching envelope, seal it and write Morris's address on the outside. I wonder how far he lives from the closest town. His farm sounds so isolated. Poor, lonely Morris. He really does need my mum.

Mum comes home several hours later. Her brown curly hair is now red curly hair. She is very pleased with the effect.

'The hairdresser said I have lovely hair, and that this colour looks very natural.'

I inspect her red hair. It has a bright luminous quality about it. 'If we have a blackout we won't need candles,' I suggest.

Mum pulls a face at me. 'Don't talk to me that way, Hatty.'

'Sorry,' I say and I really am because, hey, my mum is trying hard to look good. I should encourage her efforts.

Later I meet Suzy and Weasel and we go down to the beach. Weasel drags his towel along the road, drops his towel, loses a thong, finds it, refuses to put zinc cream on his nose, then puts it everywhere, including his hair. I can't believe the kid. It's times like this I am so happy I am an only child.

When we finally get to the beach he runs on ahead and we are totally out of our minds with joy when Suzy's mum arrives. Now Suzy and I can stroll the beach, ride a few waves, watch the cute lifesavers, hope they watch us.

We come home sunburnt, despite the layers of cream we've put on ourselves. However my pink skin pales beside Mum's new red hair.

At six o'clock on Wednesday, Raymond calls for me. I am wearing my loose jeans (I'm taking no chances) and a big sloppy t-shirt which hides those extra kilos I have put on. I run to open the door and invite him in to meet my mum.

'Pleased to meet you,' says Mum. Then she asks all the usual parent questions like what is his phone number and address so in case – shock, horror – his family decide to kidnap me, she knows where to send the police. Raymond is very patient. He nods and smiles and says the right things. I am relieved when she is satisfied and we can leave.

'Want to walk to my place or catch a bus?'

'Walk,' I say. So we stroll down the street, past the shops, past kids roller-blading and talk a bit, though not much. The air is getting cool but it's still light and I now have a chance to see Raymond properly. He is tall, quite skinny and has dark skin and eyes.

He looks serious and thoughtful.

I worry. I don't know anything much about jazz. I hope my ignorance won't spoil our budding friendship.

Raymond's house is a small cottage with little flowers and a tree in the front yard. The door is wide open and I can smell something wonderful.

'My mum's cooking a big chicken curry,' Raymond explains.

From the doorway I can hear the rumble of drums, the clear crisp sound of a clarinet, the plaintive tone of a guitar. Raymond takes me down a long corridor to the kitchen. He calls out 'Mum'. A tiny little woman wearing a green sari appears. She's very pretty and has a red dot on her forehead. Raymond shuffles from one foot to another while he introduces us. His mother, Mrs Dobie, gives me a warm toothy smile. Then I follow Raymond to a back sunroom which overlooks a leafy garden. This is where all the music is coming from.

'That's my dad,' says Raymond, pointing to the fair-haired guy playing the clarinet. Mr Dobie takes a break and grins at us, then goes back to producing this wonderful music. The other guys, a guitarist and a drummer, stand around tapping their feet in time to the beat.

'This one's called "Sweet Georgia Brown",'

Raymond says to me. 'Come on, let's sit down.'

So we squat on the floor about two metres from the group. I am fascinated. This music is good. Where have I been all my life?

'This piece is called "Honeysuckle Rose",' says Raymond as the group finishes and starts up again.

Mrs Dobie comes in and gives us a steaming plate of curry. I listen to the jazz and eat the curry. My eyes stream. The curry is very hot. I may never see again. Raymond laughs at me when I ask him to get me a glass of water so I can put out the fire in my stomach.

In between eating curry and listening to music, which is definitely stretching my musical horizons, I day-dream a little . . .

It's 1938. Warclouds are already looming in Europe. In London though, things are still peaceful. People go to work. Couples fall in love. A young woman called Harriet is learning to dance. Her dance instructor is tall, suave; experienced in the ways of life and love. He has a small pointed beard which he pulls at when he's thinking deeply. His eyes are small and shifty. He takes a special interest in his new student called Harriet. She shows promise and talent. Together they dance to the old time songs, twirling to the sounds of 'Sweet Georgia Brown'. He calls her at such times his 'Sweet Harriet Brown'. She smiles at him and dimples make small dents in her cheeks. Little does she know that he is a dastardly fiend! A Dracula in human clothing!

'Hatty, wake up!' Raymond is passing his hand up and down over my obviously blank-eyed stare. 'Do you want to dance?'

I blink at him and slowly everything comes back into focus. We put down the curry and much to the delight of Mr Dobie and his group we do a few swirls and twirls together.

When the group takes a break I say, 'You have a terrific family, and your mum's so exotic.' I think of my mum with her new flaming hair.

'My mum's from India. Dad was born in Scotland,' says Raymond.

'We're just Aussies,' I say apologetically. How fascinating if I had at least a Russian or an African in the family.

'No worries,' Raymond says.

Later his dad drives me home. In the car he whistles some old song.

'Your music was just great,' I tell him.

'Good to know that kids are getting interested in jazz again. You should hear young Raymond on the piano.'

'You play that stuff on the piano?' I ask Raymond.

'Sometimes,' says Raymond, looking out of the window. In addition to all his other good qualities, he's modest as well. Giles Conrad? Who's he?

I arrive home about nine-thirty. The street is dark and quiet. I thank Mr Dobie for the lift and Raymond gets out of the car and walks down the pathway with me. I try to think of something smart to say apart from, 'Thanks, I had a great time,' but nothing else comes.

Raymond shuffles around on his feet at the front door, puts his hands in his pockets and says, 'Uh, I'll contact you.'

I let myself inside. Mum calls out, 'Have a good time?' She's on the phone though and doesn't hear my enthusiastic answer. She's twiddling the phone cord and saying things like, 'Sure, Joe. What time, Joe?'

'Hey, remember me?' I say as I walk into the lounge room. She gives me a wave. My mum looks like a red lampshade I think, as I dump my body on the sofa and grab the TV programme.

Chapter Seven

There are first times for everything. I can remember my first day at school and the very first time I was allowed to catch the school bus by myself. Then there was that wonderful first of being allowed to go to the city without Mum trailing along.

Some of these big moments stand out in my memory like shiny lights. Others are lost in the thick clouds of time.

There has never been a first time when I have been thoroughly kissed. I've had a few guys try to grab me behind the school canteen. Believe me, they have lived to regret it. I was once kissed briefly on the lips by a nerd at a birthday party, but he did that as a dare. And there were thirty-five kids watching, so it doesn't really count.

I once had this slob ogle my boobs and then he actually grabbed one . . . this was when I was waiting to catch a bus to the city and sounds revolting and impossible, but it actually happened. He was at least twenty and I was terrified. I ran all the way home and Mum called the police but he'd run away. For all I know he's still at it, hanging around bus stops grabbing the boobs of unsuspecting girls.

That's it – all my experience. Of course, I've read novels and I've seen sexy movies and I know it all in theory. But I just haven't been kissed like, you know, a *woman*.

Suzy has. She's been kissed this way at least three times and now Giles is kissing her thoroughly and Raymond hasn't even tried with me. I've seen him three times since Wednesday and there's been lots of opportunity. I've breathed all over Suzy to check that my breath's okay. I've stared at my face in the mirror (it's not beautiful, but it's at least average). I weigh a bit more than I should, but so what! That just means I'm cuddlier. I have decided that Raymond must be very shy. I shall have to make the first move otherwise we could stay like this forever – and I'll never be thoroughly kissed.

I also have a special venue in mind for the big moment. Bondi Beach. It's perfect. People are always standing around kissing and carrying on, and the setting would make it a special first. Silky sand sliding between our toes. Waves the size of boulders crashing on the shore. In the best movies love scenes are made better by the setting. This is to be my very first time to be thoroughly kissed. I want it to be done in style.

'Want to go walking on the beach?' I ask Raymond when I phone him Sunday afternoon.

'Sure,' he says. 'But it's raining.'

'It must be a very small cloud just over your house,' I say. 'The sun's shining here.' This is a big lie, but I will come undone if it doesn't happen today. I can't bear that sick grin on Suzy's face every time she talks about Giles.

'I'll be over soon,' says Raymond. 'Just got to finish practising the piano.'

'Great!' I put the phone down. I run to the bathroom. I gargle with mouthwash. I spray 'Temptation' all over myself. I brush my hair another hundred times. It's shiny and except for that one tiny zit my skin is clear. My eyes are bright and I probably look as good as I'm ever going to look. I put on my shorts and t-shirt. Do my legs look okay or do they have 'too much meat on them'? I don't know. I'm not going to worry about it. No-one's perfect.

Meantime Aunty Sandra arrives. She and Mum sit down in the kitchen and begin to yack. Aunty Sandra leans comfortably in the chair and calls out to me, though I'm halfway in the room already.

'Oh, Hat-ty. I've got that old photograph to show you. The one of Aunt Harriet and her fiancé. Want to have a look?'

'Not now,' I say. 'I'm going to go for a walk with Raymond. Just leave it on the mantelpiece.'

Did I say that? I really am totally committed to being kissed.

I go back to my bedroom. Mum wanders in, coughs and waves the air with her hand.

'What are you trying to do – kill us all? Now, what do you mean you're going out with Raymond? You're supposed to ask me first.'

I sigh. Do all parents play this game? 'Can I go for a walk to the beach with Raymond? I'll be home in about say, three hours.'

'I think it's raining.'

'We'll probably visit Suzy then.'

Mum hesitates. She studies the lamp by my bed. She rubs her forehead as if she's deep in thought. Finally she says, 'Okay.'

Good, that's out of the way. And I've allowed three whole hours. I hope it's long enough.

Raymond turns up. His hair is wet and flat and his grey raincoat is flecked with rain. 'That cloud over my house must have grown,' he says when I open the door.

'What's a bit of rain?'

I scream out 'goodbye' to Mum and Aunty Sandra and off we go.

Raymond shakes his head. 'Want to wear my raincoat? You're going to drown.'

'I'm fine.' But the sky has sprung a huge leak. If only *that great plumber up there* would plug it. 'Let's cut across the cemetery,' I say. 'There's a shelter the other side where we can wait for the bus.'

Raymond mumbles something about going to the beach being nuts, but I'm not about to change my mind. Tomorrow it may not be so important, but I must strike now or I could wait forever.

We run between graves through the cemetery's grassy paths. At least they are grassy paths when they are dry. Right now we are running through thick brown mushy mud, spiked with tufts of grass, between tall spooky headstones. Rain dribbles down them. Suddenly I lose my balance and trip over, landing in a tangled mess beside a grave. Raymond bends over to help me up.

'I don't need help,' I growl. 'I can manage.'

His eyes have become incredibly intense. He pays no attention but pulls me to my feet. I am so close to him I am not sure whether that thud, thud I hear is my heartbeat or the patter of rain. He tilts my chin towards his. This is not what I had in mind at all. Not in a cemetery. Oh, no!

He kisses me. Then he kisses me again.

Thoroughly. Our saliva joins in a wet embrace. Then he kisses me a third time. I must taste very good because he comes back for a fourth round. His fingers play the piano as they strum a melody on my back. He touches my wet hair. I touch his wet hair.

'Maybe going to the beach isn't such a good idea,' I say finally.

He nods his head and puts an arm around me as we make our way to the bus shelter where we sit and practise more kissing. As there's no point in going for a walk, we make our way to McDonalds and sit staring at each other over a burger and french fries. Raymond has the best eyes.

'There's a jazz convention on in the University grounds soon. I'm going to play the piano. Want to come?'

He takes my hand and rubs it. I hope he doesn't notice that I bite my nails. He leans over and kisses me again. Then he puts the top of a chip in his mouth and instinctively I lean over and put the bottom half of it in mine. We both crunch on the chip, our eyes fastened on one another until . . .

French fries will never be the same again.

Later the sun comes out. Warm light trickles through the window. Raymond and I leave McDonalds and he walks me home. We kiss goodbye at the gate. Then he kisses me again.

I must be something else – the guy can't get enough of me.

When I get inside I find Mum pacing up and down the hall looking slightly deranged.

'Suzy phoned here. You didn't go over there after all.'

'We went and had a hamburger,' I say truthfully. Then I wonder . . . can she tell? Do I look like someone who's been thoroughly kissed? Is there a difference?

'You said if it rained Raymond and you were going to Suzy's house.'

'Well, we didn't go. I told you. We bought a hamburger and just sat and talked.' Honestly, she just isn't listening to me.

'Hmm,' says Mum. 'I like Raymond, but maybe it's time for me to explain a bit more about going out with boys. He's at an age where he might, you know . . . '

Mum leaves the sentence unfinished. She looks up at our ceiling. I look. There is nothing fascinating about our light fitting.

'I just wish you'd listen to me, Hatty. You've got to be careful. You're only fourteen.'

Mum then proceeds to give me a lecture about birds and bees, ewes and rams, roosters and hens. I may go crazy.

'I *know* all that stuff. All we had was a hamburger.'

My mum twiddles her red curls.

'Mum,' I ask. 'What's with you and this Joe? You're warning me but you're the one who's been living under a rock for years and years. I think we should have a talk.'

Mum glares at me. I glare at her. The phone rings. We both heave great sighs of relief. It's Suzy.

'A letter arrived for your mum from Morris. I'll bring it over.'

When I put the phone down Mum says, 'That's the shortest phone call you two have ever had. Anything up?'

'Um, no, Suzy's just going to pop over for a bit.'

I'd forgotten about good old Morris.

'Have you seen that photo of Aunt Harriet and her fiancé? It's on the mantelpiece,' says Mum, who fortunately has stopped carrying on about Raymond and the hamburger.

I'd forgotten about Aunt Harriet. I seem to only have room in my mind for Raymond and the feeling of being kissed. There is an old, slightly discoloured photo in a silver frame. I hold it up. Aunt Harriet is young and pretty. Her hair is long, way past her shoulders and is parted in the centre. Her eyes are bright and her skin soft-looking and clear. Thomas, her fiancé, is about the same height. He stands next to her, their shoulders touching. He has a hat on his head, like those in the gangster movies of the thirties. He is not facing the camera. His face is turned to one side and he's staring at Aunt Harriet and the love is just shining out of his eyes. Or at least the one eye I can see. How could he fall for someone else? They look so right for each other.

'I'm going to hang it on the wall in the kitchen facing cranky Aunt Harriet,' I tell Mum. 'It might make her feel better.'

In the kitchen, I locate that old, slightly bent nail on the wall and stand on a kitchen stool. I hoist up the new photograph. There. That looks very nice.

The doorbell rings. 'I'll get it,' I call out.

It's Suzy. We dash into my bedroom. She pulls Morris's crumpled letter from her pocket.

'You don't know how close I came to opening this,' she says, while I tear open the envelope.

I read:

Dear Margaret,

I received your letter. I was thrilled to find out that you are now a redhead. I have always loved red hair.

I don't get a chance to watch much TV here, but yes, I also like psychological thrillers as long as they are realistic.

Often one finds that life itself is one big psychological thriller. Do you know what I mean?

It seems to me that the time has come for us to meet. I am going to come to Sydney shortly and will pay you a surprise visit. As you like thrillers I am sure that you'll appreciate this.

Finally, a last small poem from me to you.

You must look swell with your red hair, Marg,
You must be quite a treat.
Adieu, au revoir, *goodbye, Marg,*
Until we finally meet.

Morris

'Oh, no,' I groan. 'I am in deep, deep trouble. What am I going to tell Mum?'

'There's something odd about this Morris guy,' says Suzy frowning. 'Why is he carrying on about your mum's hair? And you said he was shy. He doesn't sound shy to me. He sounds *off.*'

'Oh, you're totally wrong. Morris is a gentle soul. Remember he grows flowers and vegetables. He's just trying to act a bit romantic. You've got to understand. My letters have been keeping him going. There's nothing exciting about growing pumpkins and daffodils. My letters brought meaning to his life. It's just a pity Mum's going to kill me when she finds out.'

'Forget about that! What am I going to do if he turns up on my doorstep asking for your mum. Remember – he thinks she lives at *my* address!' Suzy begins to throw her arms around. Her eyes are bulging and she's looking panicky.

'No worries,' I say, though I'm starting to feel sick. 'I'm going to write to Morris this very moment. I'll tell him we've moved.'

I grab some paper and a pen, think for a moment, push aside the perfume bottle and start to write.

Dear Morris,

Please note at the bottom of this letter and on the back of the envelope my new address. Yes, I've moved – on account of Hatty's sinus trouble. The other place was too close to the ocean, so we moved to a drier street.

However, we are going away in a few days for a two-week holiday to help clear up Hatty's sinuses, so please don't write while we're gone. Also, don't come to visit me without letting me know first, so I can make the house tidy.

Suzy leans over my shoulder while I frantically write.

'You're getting really good at this,' she comments. 'Tell you what. I'll post it special delivery this afternoon, so he'll get it tomorrow. Just to be on the safe side.'

'You're a true pal,' I say as I douse the letter with 'Temptation', sign my name and write my address in big, clear print.

'This gives me time to prepare Mum. I just *know* Morris is right for her. By the time he writes again I'll have her all eager.'

'So, when are you going to tell her?' asks Suzy. 'What about now? I'm having a boring day. Giles is cleaning his dad's car and a bit of excitement would come in handy.'

'You're a sadist. No, I've got to do this carefully. Mum's stuck on this guy called Joe. I've got to find a way to talk her out of Joe and into meeting Morris.'

Then I tell Suzy that *finally* I have been thoroughly kissed. I don't tell her that the big moment took place in a cemetery. My friend has a warped sense of humour and I'll never live it down.

After Suzy leaves I go into the kitchen to talk

to gloomy Aunt Harriet. I stand up close to the wall. So close I am practically breathing on Aunt Harriet.

'I know – I've gone too far this time,' I whisper to her. 'But I'm absolutely *sure* this will all have a happy ending.'

She stares back at me, her face full of doom. I turn and face the other photograph of Aunt Harriet and Thomas. Now, they look like they understand that my intentions are good!

I go back to the lounge room where Mum sits curled up on the sofa, feet tucked under her as she reads.

'What's it about, Mum?' I ask.

'It's a science fiction book called *Time Travellers*. It's very futuristic. Really gripping, Hatty. You might like to read it.'

'Sure,' I say, thinking how much I'd like to skip the next few days, or weeks.

'Um, Mum . . . can I have a talk with you?'

'Is it urgent, Hatty?' Mum looks at me vaguely annoyed. 'I really want to find out whether the space transformer module works.'

'Um, no, it's nothing.'

This is not going to be easy!

Chapter Eight

The world comes to an end just after six o'clock a few nights later. Not everyone's world. Just mine.

I've had an early dinner. Mum's getting ready to go out with Joe. She's washed her new red hair and walks through the room brushing it. She has a brand new dress. This one is not too bad. Almost okay. It's green and shiny and shows her neckline and a bit more. Not much more, but a bit. It is loose-fitting and makes her look slim and ends at the knees.

I've tried several times to talk to Mum about how she should meet other guys. I've hinted strongly that I know someone special who's dying to meet her. She just raises her eyebrows and says, 'Really, Hatty?' Then she runs to adjust her make-up or comb her hair yet again and that's the end of that.

Tonight, while Mum checks her dress and runs in and out of the lounge room asking me how she looks, I'm watching the news. Wars, road carnage, bank holdups, the lot. I'm also thinking about Raymond ... I'm thinking about new ways to tell Mum about Morris. With all this thinking it's a wonder I'm sane. Suddenly a bolt of media lightning strikes our house, in the form of a newsreader who says in his bland, serious voice:

'Police tonight are on the lookout for Morris Melgrove, who escaped today from the Mellalong Prison Farm. Melgrove had been serving a term of two years imprisonment on the farm for marrying repeatedly without the benefit of a divorce.'

I think quickly. Marrying without a divorce? Doesn't that mean having more than one wife at the one time? Isn't that bigamy? Oh, no!

The bored newsreader carries on.

'Melgrove, nicknamed by prison inmates as "Mad Marrying Morris", was sentenced to imprisonment six months ago after ignoring warnings by judges on three separate occasions in the past when he illegally married. In his latest marrying scam he managed to deceive his four wives and twenty-seven children by working as a travelling salesman and spending several days a fortnight with each of his families.

'His multi-married life finally caught up with him when two of his Newcastle wives became friends and compared wedding photographs.

'Melgrove has been described by several of his wives as a cultured, romantic man, strongly attracted to redheads. Each of his wives had red hair. They were all shocked to find out about the existence of one another and cheered loudly when he was finally sentenced.

'Melgrove, a model prisoner at the State Mellalong Farm, is not considered dangerous. However, psychiatric reports suggest he may be mildly disturbed and should therefore be approached with caution.

'Anyone sighting Melgrove should contact their local police station immediately.'

I blink at the uninterested face of the newsreader then freeze as a photograph of Morris is plastered across the TV screen. This is insane! Can this be poetic Morris ... my mother's Morris ... *my* Morris ... sensitive, kind Morris? This can't be happening! There has to be some mistake.

'Turn down the TV,' Mum shouts at me.

I turn the sound down and dash to my bedroom. I pull out Morris's old letters and look at the address on the back. Yes, there are no two ways about it. Mellalong PF. The 'PF' must stand for Prison Farm. What am I going to do? Mad Marrying Morris? *Mad?* What exactly does that mean?

The neighbour's cat howls outside my window. I push the curtain aside and look around. It's still light. No-one there ... *so far* ... just the dumb cat sitting on the fence howling because he feels like it. Unless ... unless he's seen a stranger hanging around. What am I going to do?

'Mum!' I yell. 'I've got to have a talk with you.'

The doorbell rings. 'Go and answer it,' Mum shouts back. 'It'll be Joe. Make him comfortable. I won't be long.'

Joe? Here, already. Isn't he a bit early? Could it be Morris?

'Mum, I must talk to you.' I run into Mum's bedroom. She's putting lipstick on. I grab her arm. The lipstick smears and makes a big red line across her face.

'Look what you've made me do,' says Mum, annoyed. 'What are you waiting for? Open the door.'

The bell rings again. I bite my nails. How can I tell Mum about Mad Marrying Morris? I go to the front door and nervously peek through our spyhole. Joe's face – and it's starting to look good – looks back. He's straightening his tie.

I open the door.

'G'day, Hatty,' says Joe.

I let him in, quickly looking behind and around him. Maybe I'm being stupid. Maybe Morris is already captured and back on the farm growing cucumbers.

'Won't be a moment, Joe,' says Mum. 'Just fixing up my make-up.'

'I'm sure you look just fine without it.' Joe is being kind. He hasn't seen Mum first thing in the morning.

I bolt the door behind him.

'How are things, Hatty?'

'Um, um . . . ' I say. I feel dead worried. How can I tell Joe just how bad things are? I take him into the kitchen. 'Want a cold drink?'

'If you're having one,' Joe says pleasantly. 'My, what's that racket outside?'

'It's our neighbour's cat.'

I imagine the cat sitting on the fence minus its tail, because 'mildly disturbed' Morris has cut it off. You see, the cat is called Ginger – no prizes for guessing why.

Joe walks over to the photograph of Aunt Harriet and Thomas. 'It's not hanging right.' He looks at the back of the photo. 'It's the nail that's holding it up. It's loose. I'll fix it up next time I come over.'

There may never be a next time. We may all be dead before the night is over.

Mum wanders into the kitchen and Joe

smiles at her and gives an appreciative whistle.

'I guess we'll be off,' Mum says and she's glowing. This is my last chance.

'Mum,' I say. 'I'm not feeling too well.'

Wriggly lines crease her forehead. 'You *do* look a bit flushed, Hatty.'

'I think I'm coming down with something.' I clutch my stomach.

'Do you want to stay home, Margaret?' asks Joe. 'Hatty does look a bit green.'

The guy is a prince and to think I'd never noticed.

Mum feels my forehead. 'Hmn, you don't have a temperature. I don't know. Do you think you'll be okay for just a few hours? Joe's booked a table. We'll eat and come home. Now, I'm going to make you some warm lemon juice.'

Yuk! I should have kept my mouth shut. Mum squeezes lemon juice into a cup and adds boiling water. She makes me swallow this down with a garlic tablet. Joe stands nearby and manages to look worried. I *should* tell Mum. I really should. But the time just doesn't seem right. Surely the police have caught Morris by now. Haven't they?

I watch, in some kind of daze, as Mum and Joe leave the kitchen and walk arm in arm down our hall to the front door. Finally after numerous hugs from my mother and a note with the name of the restaurant scrawled on it in case I decide to throw up over the carpet, they leave. I am alone. Quite alone.

The house is suddenly silent. Then the cat next door howls again. I hear something tapping. It is my feet as I pad down the hall to the kitchen. My stomach growls. Maybe I *am* sick. Maybe I *will* throw up.

In the kitchen I stand there talking to grim-faced Aunt Harriet.

'You may think I had this coming, but honestly how was I to know? Anyway, I promise you this, if Mum and I get out of this okay I'll never, ever interfere in her life again.'

I hold my hand dramatically across my heart. Aunt Harriet glares at me. She just doesn't understand. In future I will talk to the other photograph of Aunt Harriet. The one with Thomas. She looks much more approachable there. I may even start talking to Thomas.

The phone rings. I jump. My nerves are so shot to pieces I can hardly think straight. I run and pick it up. It's Suzy.

My friend's voice is the same pitch as the neighbour's cat. 'I saw the news,' she shrieks. 'I saw *him*. Morris! This is too much. What are you going to do? Thank God he's got your address. Sorry. I guess that's tactless. Wow! Do you realise that you nearly had twenty-seven step brothers and sisters? Have the police come round yet? And your mum – does she want to kill you or is she keen to meet Morris? I mean – the guy *must* have something. All those wives, huh?'

I tell Suzy that Mum doesn't know yet. Suzy thinks I am either demented or in deep shock. She cannot believe I am alone at home.

'I don't think Morris has had time to make it to Sydney yet,' I say hopefully. 'Anyway, I bet the police have caught him already. I bet he's back on the farm growing more vegetables. And, it's not like he's a murderer or a bank robber. He's just romantic. He just likes to, um, marry . . .'

'And marry and marry and marry.' Suzy is still shrieking. 'Hasn't he heard about having one wife at a time? The guy's a loon who's got this thing about redheads. And your mum's a redhead. Oh, no! I think I'm going to faint.'

Which is all very well for Suzy. I am the one who should be fainting. It's my neck on the block so to speak. Well, Mum's actually. If only she hadn't dyed her hair red this would never have happened.

'I'd come over and sit with you,' squeaks Suzy, 'but what if he turns up? When the light hits my hair it gets red glints in it. Stop making those rude noises. You *know* that's true. Maybe he thinks it's time to look at younger women. You never know. Tell you what . . . I'll speak to Giles. Maybe Raymond, Giles and I will all come over. There's safety in numbers. What do you reckon?'

'I'd really appreciate it,' I say. I put the phone down and start to think. Should I call the police? Then I rationalise – surely Morris isn't going to just turn up. Soon, my best friend will arrive with Raymond and Giles. I can't call the police without first telling Mum the truth. The shock would be too much for her. Things will sort themselves out, won't they?

If that cat doesn't stop howling soon I'm going to kill it. Really, I am. If I kill it, what then? Do I get put in gaol for cat-murder? Maybe I'll end up on a prison farm like Morris, growing potatoes and pruning hedges. I think I'm going mad. Look . . . I'm wet with gooey sweat . . . My armpits must smell like an open drain. I'm feeling very, very faint and I bet I look just terrible. Raymond's coming over. What will he say? Will he think I'm a total goofball? A stinking goofball? I think I'd better stop panicking and put on some deodorant. And my hair needs brushing. Why won't that stupid cat shut up. Doesn't it know my nerves are shattered?

It seems that in the time I wait for my friends to arrive I hear creaks in the house I never knew existed. Floorboards seem to move, curtains appear to be sucked against closed windows and doors rattle. I run around checking that all the windows are locked. Good, the place is as safe as a tomb. Yuk. Did I think that?

The cat next door continues to screech. I hear a car's brakes screech. My nerves screech. I try to sit down in my bedroom, but I can't keep still. My heart is thumping so loudly I may not be able to hear the doorbell. When the doorbell does ring I leap up into the air like a jumpy kangaroo.

It could be them or it could be him. Them or *him*? I sneak to the front door and look through the spyhole. Thank goodness! It's them. The three best people in the world. I take a deep breath, unbolt the latch and undeadlock the deadlock.

Suzy's eyes are like two terrified clocks. Giles' smile is slightly crooked and he shakes his head at me. Raymond, dear sensitive Raymond, is worried. Even the zit above his eyebrow has grown. He puts his hand on my shoulder and gives it a gentle rub. Just knowing he cares makes me feel better. The three of them rush inside. Everyone speaks at once.

'We came right away. I told them everything.' (Suzy)

'I don't think this is a big deal. The guy's just a jerk. This is a waste of time.' (Giles)

'Everything will be okay.' (Raymond)

I re-deadlock the deadlock. Re-bolt the bolt. I take my dear friends into the lounge room, where we sit and talk.

'You're not making sense,' says Giles. 'You should just call the police.'

'But I don't think he'll just turn up like that,' I protest. 'And it's not like he's dangerous. Just, um, a bit disturbed. I can't call the police until I've told Mum. I don't want her to go totally off her brain. At her age, she could just drop dead with a heart attack or something. It's her hormones. I need to prepare her.'

Raymond, who has been studying the pattern of our carpet, suddenly says, 'You've got to call the police, Hatty. You really can't wait. I mean – what if he's hiding outside and your mum turns up with her boyfriend. He may think she's two-timing him. He may turn nasty. You've got to call the police now.'

Suddenly, I see it all in my mind. Joe pulls up in his car. He leaps out to open the passenger door for Mum. She gives him a soppy look. Hand in hand they make their way to our front gate, not suspecting a thing. Then from out of the bushes springs Morris . . .

This is unbearable.

'I must have been in deep shock not to think

about that,' I say quietly. 'I'm going to call the police right away.'

Suzy's eyes are shining. 'This is the most exciting thing that has ever happened to me since Weasel stuck his feet together with super glue. Should we phone the newspapers?'

I give her a dirty look. I reach for the phone and dial 000. I ask for the police and say it's an emergency. Suzy is smiling. She is getting high. Giles is looking at me like I'm a nerd and Raymond is frowning. How will I cope if he doesn't want to see me after all this? He may never kiss me again.

'Sergeant Meyer-Hoffer speaking,' a strong voice says, while I freeze inside.

'Um, um,' I say. 'It's like this . . .'

Suzy smiles encouragement. Giles says, 'Go on, tell him, you dope.' Raymond looks dead worried.

'I, um, can give you some information about Mad Marrying Morris,' I finally blurt.

'Who?' says the policeman.

'Um, Morris. You know, the guy on the news tonight – um, Morris Melgrove.'

'Exactly what information do you have?' the firm, brisk voice asks me.

'I've, um, been writing to him for a while. It wasn't my fault. He put an ad in the personal column. I pretended to be my mum and I wrote to him. I didn't know Mum would dye her hair red. Honest. I didn't. I had her interests at heart. I'm just an ordinary teenager. I've never been in any kind of trouble. The neighbour's cat has been screeching and it's true I'd like to kill it, but that's because I'm stressed out. I really wouldn't hurt a fly. A cockroach . . . maybe.'

'You're rambling,' screams Giles at me. 'You're off the planet.'

Sergeant Meyer-Hoffer says, 'Who is this? What's your name, young lady, and I really hope this isn't a hoax.'

Raymond grabs the phone.

'Her name's Hatty and she's confused. For all we know this creep is prowling outside right now. Can you send someone over?'

Raymond has taken over. What a hero he is! Just as I begin to fall apart and my legs begin to buckle, he has come to my rescue.

Raymond says a few more things to the policeman. Suzy gets me a glass of water because I must look very faint. Giles makes a rude snorting noise. Whatever Raymond says must do the trick because when he gets off the phone he says, 'They're on their way. Take it easy, Hatty.'

Take it easy! Is he kidding?

Chapter Nine

While we wait for the police to come I pace the floor. Giles deep breathes and says impolite things about the state of my brain; Suzy giggles anxiously and is glassy-eyed; Raymond goes back to studying the pattern of our carpet.

I feel like howling. The cat next door does howl, the wind outside howls. A car pulls up with a howl.

We hear the clump, clump of footsteps up the path. Then we hear the turn of a key in the lock. Is it the police using their special open-anything keys? Is it Morris using the end of a nail file? Is it . . . ?

'Yoo hoo, Hatty. It's Mum. Open up.'

Mum?

I run to the front door which I've bolted from the inside. I unbolt and undeadlock. I remove the safety latch. Mum stands there smiling like a happy tomato. Joe is beside her.

'How come you've bolted the door? Anyway,

I was worried about you. I couldn't finish my dinner. Are you feeling better, dear?'

I close the door behind them, then re-deadlock, re-bolt and attach the safety latch.

'You're very security conscious,' comments Joe, making the understatement of the century.

Mum feels my forehead. 'It's damp but not hot. I don't think there's anything seriously wrong with you, but you do look flushed.'

My gang of three meantime walk into the hall.

Mum smiles brightly. 'Keeping Hatty company, are you? That's nice.' Nobody smiles back. Joe frowns.

I hear the sound of footsteps on the path. The doorbell rings sharply. Mum turns around. 'Who could that be?' I feel really sick now.

'Police here. Open up,' a voice calls from the other side of the door.

The frown on Joe's forehead has deepened and looks like the Grand Canyon.

'What's going on?' asks Mum. She un-latches, un-bolts and un-deadlocks the door.

Three policemen, tall and official-looking, stand there.

'Does Hatty Duncan live here?' one asks. 'We're here about the call to Bondi police station about Morris Melgrove.'

'Morris who . . . ?' asks Mum.

A lifetime later the lounge room looks like the inside of Central Station at peak hour. Giles, Raymond and Suzy are sprawled out on bean bags. Two policemen are standing near the mantelpiece discussing football. Sergeant Meyer-Hoffer has perched himself on a chair beside the sofa where I am sitting. I have my hands clasped in front of me and I am trying to think of something meaningful to say because Mum is in a state of advanced shock. Her mouth is opening and closing like she's trying to find new ways to trap flies. She's also on the sofa and on the other side of Mum, on a chair he's brought in from the kitchen, sits Joe. His jaw is twitching.

Suzy occasionally cracks up giggling. When I glare at her she says, 'I just can't help it. I always giggle when I'm nervous.' Then Giles makes mean comments about me to Suzy like, 'What a prize dope, what an idiot!' Suzy, between giggles, is fascinated. She looks from face to face savouring each question and answer. Raymond continues to be mesmerised by the pattern of the carpet.

I am asked to go to my bedroom and bring out all of Morris's letters, which I do. I feel awful. I feel embarrassed. Sergeant Meyer-Hoffer reads the letters out loud. When he comes to Morris's corny poetry he cracks up. I think he is very unprofessional.

Then he reads the letter with Morris's opinion about Mum dyeing her hair red. I glance at her. She resembles an exploding traffic light.

'Is Melgrove dangerous?' asks Joe when Sergeant Meyer-Hoffer finishes reading the last letter.

'Not really, mate,' says the policeman. 'Marrying all those women without even one divorce isn't exactly legal, but he's not in the league of a hardened criminal. On the other hand, he certainly did have a thing about red-haired women. And he's been locked away for a time. He could be feeling fairly romantic, if you know what I mean.'

Sergeant Meyer-Hoffer glances sideways at Mum. Mum reaches over and clutches Joe's hand. Her eyes are like two horrified marbles. Joe pats her hand and says, 'There, there.' Then he looks at me and shakes his head.

'I think I remember reading about him a few years back,' says Joe. 'I thought it was funny at the time. All those wives and kids. It doesn't seem so funny now.'

'How did he get those awful letters out from the prison?' squeaks Mum.

'Prisoners are allowed to write letters, and of course to receive them,' says Sergeant Meyer-Hoffer. 'The whole matter would have stayed where it was – Morris writing to you,

Mrs Duncan, sorry ... um, Hatty – indefinitely, but when he heard you'd dyed your hair, Hatty, um ... Mrs Duncan, it set him off. They think he escaped in a vegetable produce truck going to town. Hid himself among the cabbages and cucumbers.'

'Gosh,' says Joe.

Mum turns to me. She's blinking rapidly and may hyperventilate at any moment. 'You, you ... Hatty, how could you do this to me? You *knew* I was going out with Joe. How could you interfere with my life?'

My mother then proceeds to tell me in a thousand different ways what a rotten daughter I am. No consideration, no thought for anyone but myself. Having a big giggle at her expense. Putting us all at risk.

'Wait a minute,' I say. 'I didn't *know* he was a nut.'

Mum starts to shake with anger. Joe's jaw twitches again. Suzy smiles. Giles mutters to himself. Raymond is frowning and keeping his eyes trained on the floor.

'Well, what are we to do, officer?' asks Joe, after his jaw has steadied.

'He's not really dangerous – just a bit odd,' says the policeman. 'He'll probably turn up with a bunch of daffodils or after-dinner mints and want to marry you, Hatty, um, sorry ... Mrs Duncan. Then again, he may get hungry and just wander back to the prison farm.'

'He's probably taken lots of vegetables from the truck,' I pipe up. 'He won't get hungry for days.'

'Be quiet, Hatty,' snaps Mum.

Sergeant Meyer-Hoffer starts to fidget and flicks through some pages of his notepad. 'Look, if it will make you folks feel better, I'll put a tap on your phone line in case he calls. Stay close to home, and don't worry. We'll get him.'

'I'm moving in,' says Joe. 'I'll look after you, Margaret. Um, you too, Hatty.'

Mum's shoulders sag with relief. She breathes out a huge sigh and smiles at Joe, then glares at me.

'You three better go along home,' she says to my friends. Suzy looks extremely upset. She's been enjoying this. Giles mutters, 'About time.' Raymond finally looks up. 'I could stay over as well, if you like.'

Raymond! What an excellent idea! Mum and I alone in the house with our respective boyfriends . . .

'It's not necessary, Raymond, thank you very much,' says Mum.

So, my dearest friends phone for a cab and then leave. I thank them profusely. Suzy thanks me profusely. She says she hasn't had so much fun since the cat got stuck on the TV aerial. Giles pulls a face and Raymond says

95

he'll be in touch. He kisses me on the cheek. My cheek tingles. It's not the same as being kissed thoroughly but comes a close second.

Sergeant Meyer-Hoffer says it's time they left. He leads the other policemen, who are still discussing football, through the lounge room, along the hall. The Sergeant gives Mum a reassuring smile and says goodbye.

Mum bolts and latches the door.

'I'll, um, bed down on the couch,' says Joe.

'You're a comfort, Joe,' says Mum. Even I have to admit that Joe is looking better by the minute.

'I'll make us all some hot chocolate,' I say. I mean, I've got to do my level best to get back in their good books. I can't live with stares and glares.

So I go into the kitchen, and get out some milk and cocoa. I'll put marshmallows in their hot chocolate. Extra sugar and cocoa. It will be the greatest hot chocolate they've ever had. They will go drunk on my cocoa. All will be forgiven.

When Mum and Joe come into the kitchen I have the cups set out on a small lace tablecloth. Joe drinks my cocoa and says it's the best. Mum just stares at me and says, 'Hmm.' I have a feeling it will take more than a cup of cocoa for her to like me again.

We sit at the table. The silence is deafening.

A door creaks. We all jump. The cat next door lets out another howl.

'I'm going to kill that cat,' Mum and I both say together.

That makes Joe laugh. 'Ha, ha, ha ha.' His shoulders jump up and down.

The Antarctic wind that has been freezing our formerly happy home lifts. Icicles melt. Mum begins to giggle.

'I'd better change the colour of my hair quickly. Maybe I'll go blonde.' Mum runs her hand through her flaming curls.

'Ha, ha,' I reply. 'Can I write to a bigamist who's got a thing for blondes then?'

Somehow, neither of them find that funny at all.

Chapter Ten

Days pass. Nothing happens. Then some jerk phones the newspaper and tells them everything. Suzy holds her hand to her heart and denies that it has anything to do with her. I have my doubts. Sergeant Meyer-Hoffer is annoyed. He had wanted to keep things quiet.

Mum books in to the hairdresser and has her hair tinted back to its original colour. Nice brown curls. Joe camps on the sofa at night. Aunty Sandra says she'd like to kill me. Mum's friend, Rosie, who must have a real problem, says that Morris sounds rather cute.

Aunty Sandra wants Mum and me to come and stay at her house. Mum gets a mushy look in her eyes and says she feels quite safe at home providing Joe is around.

Then she does something amazing. She actually phones my dad in New Zealand to tell him what is going on. She *hates* to speak to him. It brings her out in hives.

She picks up the phone, and dials his

number. She manages to speak whole sentences to Dad without one hive appearing on her face. Then she puts me on, and I have to explain everything in tiny detail. My dad huffs and puffs like an old steam engine. He is angry with me. He wants to get the next flight to Sydney. I tell him that he shouldn't be concerned. Joe's around. He's taking care of us. Dad asks who Joe is. After I explain, he says how glad he is that Mum has a boyfriend.

I realise then he's been worried that Mum has never really let go of the past. Finally, having reassured him that there's nothing to worry about (ha ha) I say goodbye.

Mum, Joe and I become instant stars. We are in all the newspapers, especially me. I am photographed talking to Sergeant Meyer-Hoffer at the front gate. A current affairs programme wants to interview us, but Mum refuses. She is very annoyed and also depressed because she has to go back to work in another ten days and she says she is so traumatised she really needs a good holiday.

Suzy phones me all the time, even though I keep telling her the line is bugged in case Mad Marrying Morris calls. I feel very inhibited when I talk to her. I mean, I'd like to tell her about my feelings for Raymond but how can I when forty-five members of the police force may be listening in. Suzy thinks this is all too much. She even says hello to the police when she calls.

'Hi, there. I'm just phoning to have a girl to girl talk with Hatty. Don't listen in. It's going to be terribly boring.'

Then she tells me all these disgusting intimate details about Giles. Honestly, I am so embarrassed.

I've even made it on TV. Imagine. They show an old photograph of me (I could swear it's one I gave to Suzy). They show a letter. It's not a letter that I sent to Mad Morris. They're in police custody now. But no-one watching knows that. It could be any letter. It could be a letter from the newsreader's mother-in-law. They show a picture of Mum (they caught her at the front gate on her way to the hair-dressers). Yes, Mum is captured in all her flaming beauty, and then they filmed her as she came out of the salon. Poor Mum. And let me tell you, everything they say about looking fatter on TV is true.

It is all extremely yuk and embarrassing. And this is what the newsreader says:

'Fourteen-year-old Hatty Duncan from Bondi, Sydney, is a key link in the search for missing gaol escapee Morris Melgrove, commonly remembered as Mad Marrying Morris. Hatty began writing to Melgrove about four weeks

ago pretending to be her mother, after Melgrove had advertised for a penfriend in the personal column of a Sydney newspaper.'

The stupid newsreader carries on and on about the whole mortifying experience. This is so degrading!

Then suddenly the heat is off! Sergeant Meyer-Hoffer tells us some fantastic news. Well, it's not *really* fantastic. I mean, the woman with the red hair in Brisbane didn't think it was fantastic at all.

'A man answering Melgrove's description broke into the house of a red-haired woman. He kissed her on the cheek while she was peeling vegetables and presented her with a carnation. That's his style.' Sergeant Meyer-Hoffer sighs. 'It's just the kind of thing he'd do. She screamed and he ran away.'

Mum says, 'So he's far away. That poor woman. Does that mean we can go back to leading normal lives?'

'Well, I'd still be careful. Keep your doors securely locked at night, and keep an eye out for him. However, it looks like you're okay for now. We're concentrating on the Brisbane area, but remember there's nothing to stop him coming down to Sydney. He's on the run. Still, he's not a big-time criminal.'

'Giving her a carnation ...' Mum muses. 'But who knows what would have happened if she hadn't screamed?'

'He's never hurt anyone, but if you're concerned why don't you stay with a friend for a week. There's a good chance someone will sight Melgrove in Brisbane, and we'll catch up with him.'

'You can both stay with me, Margaret,' Joe says gallantly.

'No offence, Joe, but your flat is hardly big enough for you, let alone the three of us.'

'What about Aunty Sandra's house?' I ask.

'Yes, we might do that. I'll have a word with her.'

Mum speaks to Aunty Sandra and it is decided that we'll move in there the following day for a week or so. I phone Raymond to tell him.

'Will you still be able to come to the Jazz Festival with the others?' he asks.

'Of course.' Raymond is so cute. And it's been such a long time since ... since the cemetery.

That night Joe decides he's going to cook dinner. He says he makes a mean bolognaise. He takes out herbs and spices and tomato puree from our cupboard, and begins to fry mince meat and onion. I am impressed.

'Didn't know you could cook, Joe.'

'I'm a very good cook,' says Joe. He has his sleeves rolled up and an apron on. He mixes this and blends that and fries this and sings. I sincerely hope that his cooking is better than his singing.

The meal is cosy. Mum and Joe make romantic eyes at each other across the table. I wind spaghetti into long swirls on my fork and drop the lot. Mum opens a bottle of wine like an expert. Joe drinks and burps. Mum drinks and burps. Sadly, I am only given enough wine to wet the bottom of my glass, but I join in the fun and burp too.

On the wall a grim Aunt Harriet looks down at us. On the other wall a younger, smiling Aunty Harriet and Thomas beam at each other. The room is filled with a kind of bolognaise warmth.

'You know,' says Mum and her eyes are shining like neon lights. 'I think it's time.'

Time?

Joe just sits open-mouthed as Mum goes into the lounge room and returns with the urn.

'Joe knows all about the earth in the urn,' she tells me. 'He knows that it's symbolic of the past and the life we shared in our old house with your father when you were younger, Hatty. I've never been able to throw out the soil from our old garden. Never, ever. Not until now.'

103

Wow! Mum's holding the urn high in her right hand, looking like the Statue of Liberty.

'I'm going to scatter the earth in our back garden.'

Joe and I rise from our seats, hypnotised by Mum's huge dramatic performance. We follow as she opens the back door.

We walk in procession onto the grass. The early evening is warm and the breeze is light. The sky is purple and birds are just winding down their songs before calling it a day. Mum opens the copper urn. She lifts off the lid, holds the urn, hesitates for a fraction of a second, then turns it upside down, shaking it in this direction and that. Earth from our old garden is scattered to the four winds.

Joe says, 'Cripes, Margaret.'

He is quite overcome by it all. I am too. This is the end of a chapter in Mum's life. The severing of the cord between that life and this. I've got to admire her. She is not pussyfooting around. She is standing tall and proud and Joe is aquiver with emotion.

I just stand there, watching them, taking it all in. Just standing there, just ... suddenly becoming frozen, totally frozen, like a Pompeii statue. Moulded. Stuck to the spot. Because, you see ... there's this man holding a long-stemmed rose leaning against the side fence.

He crosses the garden in just a few strides. Mum drops the urn. Joe's jaw starts to twitch. He grabs Mum. I grab Joe.

'Margaret?' the man says in a wispy voice.

'M-m-m Morris . . . ?' I stutter.

He tries to put the long-stemmed rose into my mother's free hand. Her other hand is glued to Joe's. Mum takes the rose because she's into heavy shock and promptly says 'Ow' because she's been knifed by a thorn.

Joe says, 'Now listen, mate. She's just not interested.'

Somehow, all the time this has been happening we've been moving backwards into the open door of the house. Joe must think he can slam it on Morris. But Morris has no intention of giving up now. As the three of us squeeze through the door and Joe reaches out a quaking hand, Morris puts his big foot inside.

'Margaret,' he says softly.

So, suddenly there we are. The four of us. In the kitchen, with the smell of bolognaise in the air and Morris Melgrove standing staring at Mum, Joe and me.

Mad Marrying Morris has droopy blue eyes. He has a little smile and fairly white teeth. There is a glazed look about him like he's gone high on seeing my mum. He looks a bit like a blue-eyed cocker spaniel. I don't know what all those other women saw in him.

'What happened to your glorious red hair?' he asks Mum.

'Well, ah, you see . . . ' says Mum.

'Now, look here,' says Joe and he tries to take a step forward, but it's hard because Mum and I are stuck to him.

Suddenly, though most of me is comatose, I manage to say, 'She went back to her natural hair colour. Look, um, Morris, it's not Mum's fault. I wrote the letters. I know I shouldn't have. But I thought your ad in the paper was really cool. I thought I'd be able to bring the two of you together. I wrote all that poetry, not Mum.'

Morris rubs his forehead and stares at me. His eyes go mushy. I may throw up.

'Hatty . . . little Hatty. How are your sinuses? How I loved that photo of your mother and you in front of the Opera House. And then that letter where Margaret said she'd coloured her hair red. Her hair. Red. And you, Hatty. Let me look at you. You look rather like my third eldest daughter. She'd be about your age.' Morris takes a step closer. His voice trails away.

Joe says, 'Listen, mate. Just be a good fellow and go back to the farm. They can look after you there.'

Morris's blue eyes fill with tears. 'I thought we had a future, Margaret. I thought we could get married. Who is this man?'

'Well, he's ah . . . ' says Mum.

'Joe,' I cut in. 'He's Joe. Mum doesn't want you, Morris. She's got Joe.'

There's a strange silence. The clock in the lounge room tick tocks. I feel rotten. I don't want to, but there's something sad about Morris Melgrove – Mad Marrying Morris – standing there with tears in his eyes. He really does love to be in love. Still, there's my mum to consider. And all those step brothers and sisters. I just couldn't cope.

Morris leans against the wall and sighs. Joe is still trying to disentangle himself from Mum and me but we are clutching him.

Suddenly, it happens. The photograph of Aunt Harriet and Thomas comes crashing down on Morris's head. That loose nail in the wall has finally given way. The glass inside the frame breaks on his scalp. Morris screams. We are so surprised we let go of Joe. He jumps forward as Morris falls to the floor. A big bump surrounded by a small patch of blood starts to grow on Morris's forehead.

While Morris lies puffing on the floor, I run to the phone. I dial 000 and at the same time scream, 'If you're still tapping this line send the police quickly. We've got Morris Melgrove holed up in our kitchen.'

It seems like hours before we hear police sirens, followed by a thumping on the front door. Police come charging into our home like fans to a heavy metal concert. It is an unforgettable scene. Joe is standing over Morris, who is stretched out on the floor of our kitchen with a bump on his forehead. The broken picture frame and photograph of Aunt Harriet and Thomas is lying beside him.

Mum is standing beside the kitchen table, half supporting herself, looking sick. The police pull Mad Marrying Morris – who is coming to – to his feet and put handcuffs on him. Joe, who has been very brave through all this, suddenly starts to twitch all over.

Sergeant Meyer-Hoffer says, 'You folks have been great. I'm, um, sorry we were misled by the Brisbane report. The trouble is you get these copy-cat crimes. Some dope heard about Morris and wanted to get in on the act. Um, you do understand, don't you?'

'No worries, mate,' says Joe obligingly.

They're ready to take Morris away, but there's something I *have* to say to him. He looks pathetic, flanked by two policemen. His blue eyes are watery and confused. The bump on his forehead is turning purple.

'I'm sorry, Morris,' I say. 'If I hadn't written those dumb letters to you this wouldn't have happened.'

Morris nods at me. The corner of one lip turns up, but the other can't quite manage it and the result is a lopsided smile.

The police lead Morris away. Sergeant Meyer-Hoffer shakes hands with everyone. The door is finally closed and we are alone.

Joe makes us all a cup of tea. I pick up the broken slivers of glass from the photo of Aunt Harriet and Thomas and put them in the bin.

'Be careful you don't cut yourself, Hatty,' warns Joe.

'Yeh, yeh,' I say.

When I lift up the photograph, a folded sheet of paper falls away from it. Huh? What's this?

'What's that, Hatty?' Mum asks.

I open the page.

My dearest Harriet, I read.

I excitedly scan the lines. At the bottom of the page I see . . .

Yours forever, Thomas

'It's a letter. A letter to Aunt Harriet. From Thomas.'

'The aunt your mother has told me about who was a nurse in the war?' asks Joe, as he pours out cups of steaming tea.

'But, but . . . how did it get here?'

'I don't know. It was your great-grandmother's photo. Don't just stand there.' Mum sounds excited. 'Sit down and read the letter.'
In a quavering voice I read:

November 6th, 1945

My dearest Harriet,

The years have passed, and yet my memory of you is as fresh as when we first met.

I know you have never forgiven me. If only there was some way I could undo the past. I betrayed you, Harriet, and I betrayed the commitment we made to each other when we became engaged. My foolish flirtation, which I must tell you was no more than just that, has cost us a lifetime together.

I have never married. I know that you are a nurse and that you recently went to work for the Red Cross hospitals in France, now that peace has been declared.

I am posting this letter care of the Red Cross in London in the hope that they can forward it on to wherever you are nursing.

I am very sick, Harriet, but before I leave this world I wanted you to know, I love you, Harriet. I always have and I always shall.

Yours forever,

Thomas

My voice cracks. Mum is dabbing her eyes. Joe is dabbing his eyes.

'Do you think she knew, Mum?' I ask. 'Do you think Aunt Harriet got this letter before she died?'

'I'm sure she did, Hatty,' says Mum and she reaches over to me and gives me a hug. 'She must have. I'd say that letter was brought back to London with her belongings after she died. My guess is that your great-grandmother, Aunt Harriet's mother, put the letter behind the photograph of Thomas and Aunt Harriet. She probably felt it was something that belonged just to the two of them.'

I stand up and walk over to the other framed photo – the grim-faced Nurse Harriet.

'You see. He really *did* love you. You were a great person. You saved a lot of lives, but you didn't have a life of your own, did you? Thomas might have done the wrong thing, but he really loved you. I just want you to know that.'

The stern, unblinking face of my aunt peers back at me.

'She knows, Hatty,' says Joe. He grabs a tissue and blows his nose. Mum grabs a tissue and blows her nose.

Honestly, the three of us are such sooks.

Chapter Eleven

It's Saturday morning. Apart from a few clouds the sky is clear. The sun is hot. The buses are full. Giles, Suzy and I are off to the Jazz Festival. Raymond has already left earlier with his dad.

Morris Melgrove is back at the prison farm growing cucumbers and roses. Mum and Joe seem to be getting serious about each other. I feel okay about that. He makes a great bolognaise.

The bus swings around curves in the road. We all hang on precariously to a metal pole. Giles and Suzy's fingers are locked together. I lose my balance and land in some woman's lap. Everyone laughs except the woman and me.

We get off at the Town Hall and then jump onto another bus.

'Do you go to Sydney Uni?' I ask the driver.

'If I went to Sydney Uni I'd be too busy to drive this bus,' replies the driver. The world is full of comics today!

We arrive at the University. It's crowded with people and cars, and even before we get off the bus you can hear trumpets and drums.

'I'm only coming to support Raymond,' mutters Giles. 'I'm not really into jazz.'

'And I'm coming to support you support Raymond,' giggles Suzy.

My friends are in goofy moods. I hope I can cope with them.

The tall buildings of the University stand around looking like they can't believe what is going on. The world of science, literature and psychology has been taken over by jazz and blues.

Different bands play in different buildings and on grassy slopes. We go from spot to spot looking for Raymond. We pass hot-dog stands, ice-cream vendors and screaming kids who have no idea why they're here. I know why I'm here. I like jazz. I like blues. All that soul stuff from ages ago. Going back to times when Great Aunt Harriet and Thomas were twirling around in London nightclubs. It makes me feel happy and sad inside. And Raymond likes it too.

Inside a big hall with bright murals on the wall we see Raymond, his dad, the guitarist and drummer. A skinny guy is accompanying them on a base which he occasionally spins around for effect.

People are sitting listening and beating time

with their hands and stomping their feet. The band's wearing striped jackets, black trousers and little hats, I think they're called boaters, on their heads. They look –

'Off,' says Giles. 'Raymond looks totally off. He looks like he's just stepped out of one of those old late night movies.'

'He looks cute. Totally cute,' I say.

'Let's sit down,' says Suzy, trying to break the icy stare that Giles and I are giving each other.

We sit near the front. The music is really something. Raymond is playing the piano, and his hands are moving up and down the notes like happy bananas. My Raymond! I feel so proud of him.

A woman comes on stage and starts singing. She's wearing a slinky, shiny dress which is so tight it looks like she's been poured into it. She throws back her head and sings. Her red mouth opens wide and out of it comes deep, plaintive words about love and loss. I feel overcome. My eyes begin to fog.

'Hello, Hatty.' It's Mrs Dobie, looking fabulous in a bright orange sari. Her thick dark hair is coiled into a bun at the back of her head. She sits next to me. Giles, of course, knows her already as she's his next door neighbour. He introduces her to Suzy.

'This music is great,' I tell Raymond's mum. She nods her head and claps time to the beat.

Suddenly the band begins to play 'Sweet Georgia Brown' – my very favourite. Raymond stops playing the piano and lets his dad take over. The clear sounds of the clarinet fill the hall. Raymond jumps over the stage and comes down to where we are sitting. People reach forward and shake him by the hand.

'Good on you,' says one fan.

Raymond pulls me to my feet. 'Come on, Hatty.' He leads me to a spot near the stage where there aren't any seats. Just enough room to dance. I hestitate for a second, but the beat of the music and the atmosphere has got to me. Raymond and I begin to twirl and spin and hold each other and I think I am in love.

The amazing thing is that other people join us. Seats are pushed to one side and soon the hall is filled with dancers. Even Giles and Suzy are shuffling around. Giles is looking like he might actually be having fun.

Later, when the band finishes up for the day, Raymond helps his dad get all their musical gear together. We make arrangements to meet later and I have strong hopes that I might be thoroughly kissed again.

Suzy, Giles and I leave and go home.

Six days and forty-nine and a half (we were

interrupted) kisses later, a letter comes in the post.

It is addressed to Mum. When she sees the name Morris Melgrove on the back of the envelope she bites her lip and says, 'Oh, no. Not again.'

I peer over her shoulder as she opens the letter. She reads:

Dear Margaret and little Hatty,

Don't be alarmed by this letter, as it will be my last. I have found a redhead who really loves me for myself. She saw me on the TV news and knew I was the man for her. Her name is Wendy and I have no doubt she is the right one for me. She will correspond with me until that magic time when I am released and we can be together forever.

One last poem to you both.

I know I drove you crazy. I know you thought me batty.
I had a thing about red hair. About you Marg and Hatty.

My life is looking better now, my future's
  looking fine.
And if I play my cards right, sweet Wendy
  may be mine.

Sincere regards,

Morris Melgrove

I laugh. 'I somehow don't think Morris is cured.'

'Anyway, I prefer Joe,' says Mum.

'He does make great bolognaise,' I say.

Mum nods her head. 'Yes, he makes great bolognaise.'

She gives me this *huge* smile. I think she's trying to tell me something.

About the Author

Moya Simons has two grown up daughters, Susie and Tammy. She lives in Sydney in a small unit with her pot plants, books and two Mexican walking fish. Moya likes marshmallows, chocolate ice-cream and Vicks VapoRub. She dislikes baked beans, cauliflower and live cockroaches (dead ones are okay).

Moya has been writing for about eight years. Her short stories have been published in literary journals and magazines. Her other books are *Fourteen Something*, *Iggy from Outer Space*, *Dead Meat!* and *Dead Average!* and they are being published in the UK, USA and Germany.

One day when she is rich and famous, she'll give up working part time in an office and write full time.

Sit Down, Mum, There's Something I've Got to Tell You was inspired by a wacky story Moya heard about a man with six wives and thirty-seven children. 'Phew!' says Moya. 'Imagine all those birthday parties.'

MORE GREAT READING FROM PUFFIN

☆☆☆☆☆☆☆☆☆☆☆☆☆☆☆☆☆☆☆☆☆☆☆☆☆☆☆

The White Guinea Pig   Ursula Dubosarsky

When Geraldine is entrusted with the care of her friend's white guinea pig, Alberta, and when that guinea pig mysteriously disappears, it is the beginning of Geraldine's growing up, and everything in her life changes.

Spider Mansion   Caroline Macdonald

When the Todd family arrive at the Days' historic homestead for a gourmet holiday, they appear to be the most delightful of weekend guests. But weekend guests should know when to leave, and the Days realise too late that silently they have become enmeshed in a spiralling web of fear.

Laurie Loved Me Best   Robin Klein

Julia and Andre share an abandoned cottage as a refuge from their lives – until Laurie, a boy on the run, arrives to upset the scheme of things.

MORE GREAT READING FROM PUFFIN

☆☆☆☆☆☆☆☆☆☆☆☆☆☆☆☆☆☆☆☆☆☆☆☆☆☆☆☆

The Other Facts of Life   Morris Gleitzman

Ben's father doesn't have the answers when the questions get tough. Ben mounts a campaign that is deadly serious and very, very funny.

Old Tom   Leigh Hobbs

Old Tom is a lovable, battle-scarred, naughty but wickedly appealing old tom cat. Here are his adventures, told with a witty text and hilarious illustrations!

My Grandmother   Barry Dickins

Marvellous anecdotes about a magnificent character: the author's grandmother, at ninety-eight, survived independently with a pramful of money and a tough outlook on life.

MORE GREAT READING FROM PUFFIN

☆☆☆☆☆☆☆☆☆☆☆☆☆☆☆☆☆☆☆☆☆☆☆☆☆

The Girl With No Name   Pat Lowe

When Matthew goes camping at Goanna Gorge in the Kimberleys he's determined to find the ancient rock paintings he knows are hidden there. But his plans fall apart when he realises he cannot find his way home . . . until he meets the girl with no name.

Mullaway   Bron Nicholls

Mully finds herself in charge of a muddled household when her mother has to suddenly and permanently take to her bed, and discovers startling truths about each of her family.

Now a feature film.

Stormy   Mary K. Pershall

It had all started long ago, when her mother was still in their house. One awful afternoon, Stormy's dad had lifted her onto the big white mare and said, 'Ride. Ride till someone takes you in.' But this summer, Stormy's had enough of being dumped. She wants to be with people who have her blood in their veins, and she's determined to make it happen.

MORE GREAT READING FROM PUFFIN

☆☆☆☆☆☆☆☆☆☆☆☆☆☆☆☆☆☆☆☆☆☆☆☆☆☆☆☆☆

Ganglands   Maureen McCarthy

The dramatic story of the summer when Kelly leaves school –
when she will be faced with the toughest decisions of her life.
Set in the cultural melting-pot of inner-city Melbourne, from
the author of the *In Between* series.

Out Of It   Maureen Stewart

Clayton's never been into drugs but when Carrie Brown agrees
to go to the school formal with him and suggests that they get
some 'gear' for the night, he decides to try whatever's
offered . . .

Played Out   Damian Morgan

Andrea Quill is fifteen, a junior tennis champion, already
number three in the world, and the Ace Tennis Squad's ticket
to fame. That is, until her steel-cold determination seeps away
and even her coach can't keep her on the court.

MORE GREAT READING FROM PUFFIN

☆☆☆☆☆☆☆☆☆☆☆☆☆☆☆☆☆☆☆☆☆☆☆☆☆

Love Me, Love Me Not Libby Gleeson

Relationships. Feelings. For the ten Year Eight students who are the central characters in *Love Me, Love Me Not*, it is a time when little else matters. Nine separate stories or one longer tale? Judge for yourself how this new work by award-winning author Libby Gleeson can be read.

Shortlisted in the 1994 CBC Book of the Year Awards.

Lovebird Peter McFarlane

From the author of *The Flea and Other Stories* here is a powerful new collection of unforgettable characters.

A Children's Book Council of Australia Notable Book, 1994.

Bittersweet Toss Gascolgne (Ed)

Stories about love, relationships and heartache from Australia's most popular and award-winning authors.